GAME OVER, ShrinkWithers!

GAME OVER, ShrinkWithers!

Sarah Ray Schwarcz

S. Schwarcz

To All . . .

*Who dream of making a difference and
help others achieve their dreams.*

*Who place books in our hands and say,
"I know you'll love this!"*

*Who understand our world belongs to everyone,
and we must take good care of it.*

*Imagination sings grand melodies
in our hearts and minds.*

Sarah Ray Schwarcz

*We can make a difference in keeping our
treasures of forests, fields, and resources
protected when we devote our time and energy
to conservation and innovation.*

"When we plant trees, we plant the seeds of peace and hope."

Wangari Maathai PhD
Kenyan Environmental Activist; 2004 Nobel Peace Prize;
Founder, Green Belt Movement

"It is our collective and individual responsibility . . . to preserve and tend to the world in which we all live."

14th Dalai Lama of Tibet

"Earth is what we all have in common."

Wendell Berry
Novelist, Poet, Essayist, and Environmental Activist

"The best time to plant a tree was twenty years ago. The second-best time is now."

Chinese Proverb

"We do not inherit the earth from our ancestors. We borrow it from our children."

Native American Proverb

"The greatest threat to our planet is the belief that someone else will save it."

Robert Swan
OBE (Order of the British Empire) Environmentalist;
Founder of 2041 Foundation,
for the preservation of the polar regions;
First person in history to walk on both Poles

Table of Contents

1

The Telling

Jenny opened the front door at 3:30 p.m. on Friday, tossing her red backpack into the living room, landing it on the coffee table instead of the comfy chair. She was excited to have no homework and only one week of school left.

Dachshund Winnie sprang up from his nap by the couch and scrambled to greet her with slobbery kisses. Jenny crouched to scoop him up and raced to the kitchen to find a snack. She slid to a sudden, squeaky stop, shocked to see her mom and dad talking in whispers, frowning at a letter sitting on the counter.

Their faces. She knew something was strange.

Usually good at reading faces, Jenny couldn't decide if Mom was excited or worried. She smiled, but her mouth quivered. It was odd for Dad to be home at this time of day. Mom motioned Jenny over, pointing to the letter.

Dad began reading the letter aloud. Jenny could feel them watching her with a third eye—the extra eye parents have that sees all, knows all, and catches you every time you try to hide the truth. And today, it looked like Mom and Dad were trying to hide some truth.

Winnie wiggled in her arms; he could sense she was anxious. Jenny struggled to stay calm, but she felt something awful was about to happen. Did Dad lose his job? Were they going to move again? Was someone sick? She should have been excited to hear she was selected for the training games this summer. But Dad and Mom's faces looked so worried. She couldn't pay attention to all of the letter's contents.

Dear Mr. David Cranston, Mrs. Meg Cranston, and Ms. Jennifer Cranston,

We are pleased to inform you we have selected JENNIFER to compete in the training TriTopTechRun Games, starting in upstate New York on June 15th. The enclosed packet details the items JENNIFER must bring to training camp. Pack only those things listed. Any items not on the list will be removed, including food, toys, phones, and electronics. Your son / daughter will be supplied with all necessary game electronics, materials, phones, and survival items.

Your signatures below will indicate you and your child agree to ALL terms of the competition. Your family will be bound to the TTTR Rule of Silence. During the training period, any observed attempts to communicate with anyone outside the competition will be grounds for immediate dismissal. Upon completion of the competition, your memories will be wiped clear.

We realize this competition and its rules are extremely challenging for children and parents. The importance of this competition for our world's environment places an enormous responsibility on those chosen to compete. The ShrinkWithers have been doing great damage. We must defeat them. We trust that your talents, interest, and commitment will see you through as we enter this First-Lap Training Period.

If you have any doubts about your child's suitability or any other concerns, it would be best to break off this relationship now, prior to further involvement. Be certain to fill out the Withdrawal Form if you do not intend to compete.

Remember, your next step is to open the TTTR Direction Packet, go through it carefully with

JENNIFER, fill out all forms, then mail them back by certified mail. We await your response.

Good luck! Welcome to TriTopTechRun Games. You're a WINNER!

> *Andrew H. Bingham, PhD*
> *AstroSPAN Chief of Operations*
> *TriTopTechRun Game 2*

"Jennifer Elizabeth?" Her dad spoke first when he finished the letter. He smiled for the first time since she'd arrived home.

Jenny set Winnie down on the floor and straightened up to her full Jennifer Elizabeth height and waited.

"Jennifer Elizabeth, it has come to our attention . . ." He paused.

Jenny calmed down a little when she heard her whole name. It was a game she and Dad played. Jenny knew that in most families using your full name means you are in trouble. In Jenny's family it meant, "You're almost a grown-up, and I value your opinion." He knew she loved it when he pretended she was almost an adult. It always made her try a little harder and stand a little taller.

"Enough! Just blurt it out." Mom couldn't take the suspense any longer. She and Jenny had a lot in common, especially impatience.

Dad cleared his throat. "Jenny, I've accepted a unique assignment in upstate New York for the summer. While you're in the training camp, we'll be nearby. But we won't be able to travel to the cousins, like we planned."

Jenny interrupted. "No! You promised Branch and me, Dad. This summer was going to be our best ever. We were supposed to be free to hang with our friends in June and July, and in August we're going to our cousins in Ohio. We had plans. You can't change them. Now you're telling me I have to be in the tech games, and we'll be out East, but you'll be working, instead of our vacation."

Winnie hovered near her feet, knowing she was upset. He was on full alert, his ears back, his dark eyes watching her closely. When Jenny began shouting, Winnie started whining.

Mr. Cranston's work often took him out of state in the summer, as he tried to bring government and local agencies together to share new climate change strategies and design technical advances. Summers were especially complicated because of his work schedule. This wouldn't be their first ruined summer. They didn't travel much.

He had spent many years of strategic planning in a think tank made up of engineering, chemistry, physics theory, and computer research professionals. They approached Earth's climate change issues by bringing some of the great scientific and corporate minds together to create virtual models to simulate their theories.

After several years of working with adults, the first TriTopTechRun competition to invite talented children was held last year to explore options to combat global resource pollution and depletion before it was too late. Knowing his children possessed some skills that might be useful in the coming decade, Dave had entered their names in the lottery for last year and again this year. He didn't tell anyone, in case they weren't chosen.

Dave spit out his words fast, deciding to get it over with.

"We're moving out there next week," he said, "and you're coming with us. Like in last year's competition, you'll continue your student training in the TriTopTechRun experiment outside of Branson Village, New York, up in the northeast corner of the state."

This certainly was not what Jenny had expected. Jenny stopped, took in a big gasp of air, let it out with a snort, and started her Gramma's toe wiggling chill-out strategy. It didn't work. Jenny braved on anyway, looking back and forth from her mom to her dad, searching for any teensy sign of normal. They were so worried about her, they had lost their usual neutral expressions. Everything was different today. They looked frazzled.

"When we finished last year's competition, they said another would take place *in a few years*. Why is it happening again so soon?"

Jenny could tell her dad wasn't as sure of himself as he usually was. Each time she asked a question, it took him longer to answer. Something was odd, definitely odd.

"We'll come back after a couple of months. I'm not sure how long my assignment will take."

"When do we have to go?"

Dad couldn't look Jenny in the eye when he answered. "Tomorrow."

That makes no sense. The letter states the TriTop will start on June 15. Why did Dad say we're leaving tomorrow? Shocked, Jenny pressed both hands on the top of her head. All this information, like being hit with a ton of bricks. She had so many questions.

She wanted to collapse on the floor in a sniveling Branch-throws-another-tantrum heap. She wanted to kick and scream and shout. *But if I crumple to the floor, I would be just like my brother, Branch. And the big-girl-Jennifer I want to be would shrink down to little-kid-Jenny.*

Jenny took another deep, wheezy breath and blurted out a run-on stream of anxious thoughts.

"What about Branch? He's only ten. We're still in school. What's he going to do next week without us? Who will help him with his homework, and help pack his backpack in the morning, and teach him how to survive the playground monitor who tries to keep kids from having fun, and microwave his supper when Mom can't make it home in time before we starve to death, and walk him to the corner to catch the bus, and take him across the street to Mrs. Snyder to babysit, and . . ."

Jenny was out of air but kept going, listing the many chores she always had to do for Branch, all those things she usually despised. Now they seemed like fun. Now they made her feel warm and safe and comfortable. She grabbed Winnie off the floor and hugged him tightly, trying to calm down.

"Plus, my twelfth birthday is next week, and everyone's coming, and it's not fair!"

Seeing Jenny becoming hysterical, Dad cut her off. "We know, Jenny. We know. This won't be forever. Only a month or two, until we complete this year's service and we've made a difference. Then we can live like a normal family again, at least for a while. Trust me, it will seem like a short time. It'll fly by. I promise."

He was talking fast again. He managed a slit of a smile at the corner of his mouth to reassure her.

"You know, like last year, your training is so intense and takes up seven days each week. It will be impossible to come back to celebrate your birthday."

Jenny tried to keep her cool on the outside, but her mind was doing somersaults inside. Her mouth felt like she had shoved a whole cotton candy fluff ball in it—except cotton candy always melts in your mouth. This information just stuck there. It felt like that gray gunk that whirls inside the window of the vacuum cleaner.

She waited for Dad or Mom to tell her more. She counted to twenty. They were silent. They must have decided they'd given her enough of a shock for one evening, so they told her she should take her favorite sci-fi novel upstairs and read until their meal was on the table.

After giving them her angry Jennifer-Elizabeth-is-going-to-throw-a-frantic-fit look, she shoved her book under her arm, grabbed her scruffy Archibald Bear for company, and ran out of the kitchen. On her way up, she stomped hard on the first four stairs so they'd realize just how upset she was.

Then it all hit her, and she spun around and shouted at the top of her lungs, "Why can't we be like a normal family?"

They didn't even bother to answer.

* * *

While they ate, there was no more talk about the competition. After dinner, Jenny went to her room and read another fifty pages before she fell asleep. She was thankful it was a fantastic book with her favorite characters who distracted her from the usual fears of slurping green monsters who snooze and smile toothily under all kids' beds.

The familiar sounds of Mom and Dad finishing the dishes, closing the blinds, and checking the door locks were comforting, helping her pretend all was normal. Jenny knew Branch had late soccer practice on Wednesdays, so she didn't miss him at supper, but she wished he'd get home before she fell asleep so she could warn him about their parents' plans to crash their summer. Again!

Winnie, worn out from all the drama tonight, curled up next to her on his own little fuzzy pillow. Keeping his people happy was a very tiring job some days.

Usually, Mom and Dad came in a few times to tell her to turn off the light and go to sleep. They didn't come in tonight; maybe they couldn't handle any more questions. She'd forgotten to ask one important question.

Who entered me in the contest for this year's competition? She clearly remembered telling her parents after last year's games that she didn't want to lose her summers again, and they had nodded. *Why have they changed their minds?*

It took forever, but Jenny finally passed out, right after her last thought. *Where was Branch tonight; shouldn't he be home by now? Soccer practice never lasts this long.*

2

The Questioning

The next morning, in that half-awake stage right before opening her eyes, Jenny vaguely remembered it would be much safer to stay asleep. She scrunched her eyes tightly shut and pulled her softest pillow over her ears. Something about yesterday bordered on disaster, but she couldn't think what.

She remembered. She sprang upright. Winnie bounded off the bed and ran downstairs to be let out.

Her bedroom looked the same, but it didn't feel the same. The bed looked the same, but even Archibald seemed to have a startled wrinkle on his forehead. Or was it her imagination? She couldn't think of what to do, what to say, what to ask. She wanted to back up—back up to yesterday. *Before* the letter.

"Jennifer, are you awake?"

Torn between pretending to still be asleep and saying, "Yes, I'm up," to face the day, she chose "Yes" and waited.

Mom shouted, "Take a quick shower, dress, and come down."

The warm shower helped her wake up and improved her dreary mood.

Stepping into the kitchen, Jenny regained her courage when she smelled bread toasting, bacon sizzling, and coffee bubbling.

"Okay, that was all a dream yesterday. Right, Mom? Just a dream. Right? You and Dad always like to play jokes on me. Tell me it was a joke?"

"I sure wish it was, Jenny, but nope. As soon as you can get into your positive mood, we'll do what we always do when something difficult faces our family. We pull ourselves together and deal with it. Right?"

Mom's voice sounded calm, but she dropped a piece of toast on the floor and forgot to turn off the faucet. Jen noticed she opened and closed the refrigerator door several times but took nothing out of it.

Winston scratched at the door to be let back in. Jenny put his food in his bowl and waited for him to gobble it down before picking him up and returning to her seat.

Dad bounced into the kitchen, looking more cheerful than last night.

"Almost ready to go? Let's eat and get started. I'll give you lots more details. You and I will go shopping for things we'll need for our challenge before we're on the road. Today will be your day to ask me questions, but I don't know much more than you do. I know that's hard to believe, but true. We have to prepare carefully and grab each precious minute when it's available."

Dad had regained his usual upbeat tone, but it was hard for Jenny to focus and believe everything would turn out okay.

His words said everything would be fine, but Jenny felt he was hiding another message, something secret but much more important. She couldn't translate his parent code this time. It made her feel out of control. While he was talking, she spaced out.

Jenny did what she always did when things overwhelmed her—she cocooned into her imagination. She felt her body deflating, as if all her "happy helium" had left and she was shrinking into herself, into her mind. She thought she might blow away soon, through the window, across the patio, out of the yard, and down the street, never to be seen again. Landing in the middle of the Magic Kingdom at Disney World, dressed as Cinderella, with Pinocchio on her right side and Goofy on her left. Strange feelings of separation took over. Jenny always had one foot in the real world and one foot in fantasy land. Her vivid imagination served her well in both worlds.

Perhaps I shouldn't have eaten all that chocolate at school yesterday.

Suddenly, she stopped. She hadn't heard or seen Branch this morning. Usually, he was annoyingly close to her, following her everywhere, being as irritating as possible. He always stuck to her like glue until she could wave him away. *What happened to that horrible gurgling sound he makes when he brushes his teeth and spits everything all over the counter instead of in the sink? I didn't hear it this morning.*

"Mom, where's Branch? Still in bed? How come he doesn't have to get up if I do? Should I go wake him?"

Dad and Mom gave *that look* to each other. You know, the one that says they really wished she'd not ask questions, and she better stop because they were not going to answer.

"Jennifer, we need to focus on our tight schedule today. Branch will be down in a minute, I'm sure. Not to worry."

It was happening again today. Mom's words and face didn't match. Her words said *not* to worry, but her face had worry stamped all over it—solemn eyes, frown above the eyes, mouth straight across. Not even a hint of an "everything's okay" smile.

Seriously? Seriously? Do they think I'm not noticing something weird—something even stranger than all the stuff they told me last night? Jenny waited for one of them to pick up the pieces of her brain and heart and set them back in place. Moms and Dads don't realize kids can read their minds by what they *don't* say as much as by what they *do* say. She was glad to have Winnie on her lap. Petting him helped her stay calm.

The toast popped after its third reheat cycle, smelling burned, but they were hungry and started eating. Dad moved his chair closer and put his arm around Jenny, giving her shoulders his best soft hug. For her entire life this had always worked to make her feel better. It did nothing for her today. Cozy had turned to crazy.

Everyone was silent as they ate their breakfasts, looking down at their plates. There was no eye contact. Dad decided it was time to open a conversation.

"Remember about a year ago, when you were in fifth grade? I had to go out of town for a while, and you and Branch and Mom went up north to stay in that cabin for most of the summer. Well, that wasn't just a vacation. I took you there to keep you all safe while I was working for my job with NSFF, National Security Field Forces. My duties caused some terrible people to threaten our family's safety, in order to defeat me and destroy the project I was designing. We needed to separate in order to be safe, so I took you guys up north, and then I went out east. My superiors cleared the danger, and we were safe enough to return to our home after a while."

Jenny took in this information, but she was so worried about Branch, she wasn't really listening. She hadn't seen him last night or this morning. Mom and Dad were avoiding her questions.

"Dad, why isn't Branch down yet?"

That Mom-Dad look traveled from eye to eye again. Jenny noticed a slight shake of Mom's head, but Dad broke in and started talking fast. She had to forget about Branch in order to hear what Dad was saying. Winston was getting wiggly, so she set him down, and he did his usual circle around the kitchen, searching for any breakfast crumbs for his doggy-dessert.

"After we returned home, we noticed you seemed to know what we were going to say, almost before we said it. Mom and I talked and figured it was just that you were so smart and very good at thinking things through—way above your age level. But then we also realized that you could 'fix' things in an instant. Remember, on our way back, the roads were icy? We had stopped to get gas and put air in our tires. As I was filling our tank, a car ran into the pump next to ours, and the gas nozzle broke off, spraying gasoline out of the pump and onto the concrete. You rolled your window down and turned around to look at the mess. As we watched you, we saw the nozzle somehow get back on the hose. The gasoline stopped gushing. It looked as if there had been no accident.

"There was no gas left on the ground. It had all disappeared. We were in a hurry and just shook our heads, trying to forget about the whole thing. But it sat in our minds that something strange had happened. We were puzzled but had no time to think more about it. We were too busy that night with the dangerous weather and roads."

"Yes, I remember, Dad."

"That was just the first of several strange occurrences last year. Dangerous things would happen, and whenever you were near and turned to look, the disaster would become undone, as if nothing had occurred. And when we would ask you about the incident, you seemed fuzzy about what had happened. I think it bothered you.

"You talked about it to Branch. He was very upset. He came crying to us that night to tell us there was something creepy going on with you— because you thought you had super powers and could fix serious things, like car accidents, school grades, and almost everything, just by *wishing* them away!"

"Yes. I told Branch I thought I could change things back to the way they were before an accident or disaster, and you called me down to talk with you and Mom and Branch. But when I came down, Mom signaled me behind Branch's back that I should say Branch wasn't telling the truth, and I should deny everything. I thought you and Mom had gone off your pancakes then because up until that time you always told me I should tell the truth, the whole truth, and nothing but the truth.

"And there you were, telling me to hide the

truth from my brother. You always told me to act like his role model and be a good example of truth and honor. I became one very confused kid that day. Dad, where's Branch?"

"In a minute, Jenny, in a minute. Let me finish here."

"Enough already!" Jenny exploded to make sure her parents understood she'd had enough of the stalling, the quiet faces, the lack of answers, and the promises that everything would be okay. Most of all, they needed to know she could no longer ignore the fact that something might seriously be wrong with Branch.

They are hiding something from me. I've asked three times. Jenny put her hands out in front of her, palms up. She ran out of the kitchen and up the stairs, toward Branch's bedroom. Winston scampered up the stairs after her, his short legs doing their best to keep up.

3

Hiding

Jenny had reached the halfway point in her race up the stairs to find Branch when she heard her mom's horrendous scream. She jerked to attention on the landing, not knowing which way to go. Should she run up the stairs to check on Branch or down to find her mom? The scream shocked Jenny back to reality and made her desperate to get to her mom fast.

Jenny stood still and waited for another scream. No sound. Winston stood still, waiting for Jenny to move. He followed Jenny as she bolted down the steps and galloped into the kitchen. No Mom. The next noise she heard was the screech of tires and the roar of a car engine. She glanced out the dining room window in time to see a dark-blue SUV speeding out of sight.

"Mom? Dad!"

No answer. Jenny ran through the dining room, took the stairs two at a time, and checked every bedroom and the bathroom. Nothing. Winston had used up all his morning energy and waited at the bottom of the stairs. Jen grabbed her cell phone from her bed and dialed her mom. It went to voice-mail. Next, she dialed her dad's number. Voicemail.

We were all together only a few minutes ago. Where are they?

A tiny thought formed. *They always tell me I have this special ability to see things before they happen, or once they do happen, to reverse them. That's it! I'll try to back up everything to before Mom and Dad went missing.*

Jenny sat down at the top of the stairs, closed her eyes, and stayed still, concentrating on seeing Mom and Dad in the kitchen, talking while they ate breakfast. Nothing happened. Jenny squeezed her eyes tighter, trying to get into her brain, to make time back up. Nothing.

This wasn't working.

Just my wishful thinking. I feared it wouldn't work since these strange back ups have usually happened without my control. What do I do now?

We practice Dad's fancy emergency drill responses for many things, but not for Mom and Dad disappearing at once, in a single moment, from our own house, with the sun shining and the breakfast smells still in my nose, and Branch nowhere to be seen.

Suddenly, she heard a loud voice coming from the porch.

"She must be here someplace. Our infrared camera showed us three people and a dog inside. Take the stairs. Check the bedrooms and the windows. Hurry!"

Jenny grabbed Winnie and dived across the upstairs hallway, squeezed under her bed, felt around on the floor under the head of the bed, and found the latch that lifted a hidden door in the floorboards. It opened to a tiny space in the floor, under the bed. Just big enough for a kid her size and a small, squished dog. They slid down into the area and lay very still.

Her phone rang. *Turn it off, quick! Breathe. In-2-3. Out-2-3. In-2-3 . . .*

She heard two sets of heavy footsteps running up the stairs. *This is when I shouldn't breathe at all . . . so they won't find me.* Winston had never sat so still for so long. He must have sensed something was really strange.

Not a muscle moved in her body. She went into one of her slow-down-think-first trances. Doors opened, then slammed shut, one after another. *They'll be in my bedroom in a few seconds.*

Don't breathe. Not a single inhale. You can do this, girl. You've got this. You've got to get this! Yikes! They said three people in the house, not four. Where's Branch?

The bedroom door shot open, banging hard against the wall, opening up the ugly doorknob hole in the wall that always needed patching.

"This looks like her room. See those posters of Iron Man and Wonder Woman on the wall? Yeah, this has to be it. Check the closet, Mark. Move everything!"

They rummaged through her closet, grumbling as they went.

If they find me, I'm done for. They appear to be looking only for me. Why aren't they asking where Branch is, if they know so much about my family? Then she knew. *They must already have Branch!*

Panic, along with a desperate need for more air, grew like a hungry gremlin in her chest. *Calm down.*

"She's not in here! Check the bathroom. Quick. We've been here too long. Next, we'll do the basement. Hurry, Kyle!"

If she could last a few more seconds, she'd be able to take a deep breath. *I can do this.* She heard them slam the bathroom door and head down the stairs. *Maybe I could escape while they're in the basement. I'll wait.* When she heard the side door open next to the basement stairs, she decided it was time to make a run for it.

Jenny didn't trust that they were finished inside the house but couldn't let any more time pass before trying to locate her parents, even if her own safety was now at risk.

Now or never! She gulped oxygen, grabbed

Winnie, pushed open the wood-slat floor door, stayed low to the ground, and took a second to listen. *I know they're still in the basement. Now! Make a run for it! Go! Go! Go!*

She ran—across her bedroom, down the stairs, two at a time, and out the front door. Winnie didn't make a sound.

4

Pleading

"I caught her!"

A grumpy giant guy grabbed Jenny's arm the instant she flung open the front porch screen door. He must have circled around the house. She kicked. She screamed. She scratched. Winston barked and nipped at the guy's feet but was not able to scare him off. He left to go find some help. *Where are the nosy neighbors when you need them?*

A second guy came around the corner of the house and stood watching. He was smaller than the man holding Jenny, but he looked just as menacing.

"Mark, need me to help ya?"

At least now I know the name of the brute holding me. He sure doesn't need help because I'm not making any progress trying to get out of his grip.

While Jenny squirmed to escape, she checked up and down the street again. *Strangely quiet this morning.* A light rain was pattering down. Grumpy Giant Guy Mark and she struggled, but he was so much bigger, it took little energy for him to hold her. Her punches were falling on his enormous arms but doing no damage.

There were so many houses and apartment buildings packed tightly on their block, surely a neighbor could see she was in trouble. Parents leave early for work, and most kids walk themselves to the bus. Ten minutes more and there would be lots of kids heading to the corners, with a few kindergarten moms hugging goodbye.

If only Winnie and I had stayed tucked under the bed, they would've left without finding me.

These guys were rough, but they seemed not to want to harm Jenny. It was just that they were so much bigger, no action she made had any effect.

I'm not in control. I have to change my tactics. It's time for my sweet-little-girl-please-help-me-sir approach, and maybe some bluffing.

"Please! Please! Don't take me anywhere. My mom and dad will be back shortly, and if they don't see me here, they'll be terribly sad, and they have lots of friends, tons of them, friends in high places. Friends with fancy suits, body armor, big black SUVs, all that stuff." Jenny was using her knowledge of television shows to fill in her threats. She knew her parents had no such friends.

"Things will go badly for you if you don't release

me. What's going on? You're making a big mistake. If you let me go right now, I promise to report how nice you were, and maybe you won't be in so much trouble."

I was using my fast-talking-reasonable-Jennifer voice now. You know, the one that never works with your parents but might work with strangers because they don't know all your tricks.

"Sure, little girl, sure. We took on all this trouble, and we have no orders to carry out. And we're just going to smile at you and tiptoe quietly away. How dumb do you think we are?"

I decided it was best not to answer this question truthfully. Especially because I noticed he had a name badge on his shirt pocket. *What bad guy wears a name tag? I guess a guy named Kyle does.*

"We have friends in high places, too. Our friends are in control now. Our friends want you to be brought to them ASAP, so keep quiet. Stop resisting, and let's go."

They escorted her from the porch to their car, walking her along, wedged tightly between them, each with one hand on an arm. Her screams were useless because Kyle's smelly onion bagel hand covered her mouth. When they threw her into the back seat of the SUV, she heard all four door locks click. Mark pulled away from the curb.

Jenny was glad Winston had escaped and hoped he could find a neighbor who knew him and would take him back home and discover something was very wrong.

I can't believe no one is outside of their houses. Not a single person. No kids. No one.

Kyle sat next to her, gripping her hands behind her back, but the minute they got in the car, she broke loose and continued to pound him. Her sweet-talking-little-girl act had failed, so she went back to her best power-punch maneuvers.

"Get her out of the car and throw her in the trunk. Don't hurt her!" Mark snapped at Kyle.

"How do you expect me to get her in the trunk without hurtin' her? She keeps kickin' and scratchin'. I can't hold her without hurtin' her, and she's hurtin' me because I'm holdin' back."

"Well then . . ."

"No! We were told no hurt, no bruises, or there will be no Kyle and no Mark. Besides, I don't hurt kids . . . Never did . . . Never will."

"Okay," Mark mouthed silently. He hesitated, then turned back to Jenny, who was still in a tight hold.

"Okay, Little Missy, just a minute here. You know we got orders, and you know we have to take you with us, and you know we haven't hurt you one little bit, so you gotta help us out here. Let's just pretend this is gonna end well, and we get paid, and you get to see your parents and your little brother. Isn't that what you want? To find your family?"

Brother. The magic word.

She quit struggling for a minute to think things through and try to figure out what to do next.

Brother! Finally. I knew it. They have Branch, as well as my parents. Why didn't Mom and Dad tell me Branch had been taken? They must have known last night. Why did they pretend nothing had happened? Now I understand why their faces looked so worried yesterday. Now I see why Dad had to move up the date of us going. He's headed out to try to find Branch.

I'll play along. These guys hold all the cards right now. I'll have to wait until it's my deal. How dare he call me Little Missy!

Jenny pretended to relax; she even managed a smile and released her fingernails from Kyle's bulky, hairy arm. *These jerks won't know it's only my sneaky-Jenny smile—the one I use whenever I trick Branch into doing our worst chores, like sweeping up the dog hair and finding lost Legos under our couch cushions.*

"Sure. I'll calm down. I'm supposed to trust you guys to get me to my family? Are you kidding me? Nothing you two have done so far makes me believe this is a win-win. Maybe in the movies, but not here. You've stolen me from my house. You've grabbed my parents and my little brother—kidnapped them and taken them to who knows where—and I'm supposed to trust you now?"

As he listened to Jenny's insults, Kyle scrunched his big fingers into a fist and looked like he wanted to hit her.

"You know, none of us are happy with this. We have pressure from people above. I sure bet you're scared out of your little mind, Missy. But so are we."

I can't believe he's doing it again. Missy, my eye!

Jenny decided to change her tactic. She smiled and said, "Okay, I trust you. I'll stop fighting. Don't throw me in the trunk. I get dizzy when I can't see out a window. If I'm dizzy, I throw up and everything will be a big mess. I'll just sit here, real quiet. I promise to be good."

"We don't trust you to sit here quietly. You'll still kick and pinch and scream, and we've got several hundred miles to go before we stop." Kyle sounded tough, but he was softening. He looked her straight in the eye in the rearview mirror and said, "Honest?"

Kyle stared at her before he finally decided to slide out the back door and move up to the front. He snapped the four-door lock shut so Jenny would be powerless to escape. Mark stepped on the gas pedal and gunned off, their precious package safely confined.

"Honest. But I still don't trust you to get me safely to my family. How do I know you'll keep *your* promise? Where are we going? Maybe if you tell me where we're going, I can trust you."

"Well, now, little Missy. You don't know, and we ain't about to tell ya, but since we're a lot bigger than you, you have to trust us. You have no choice."

Mark spoke in a calm tone now, which gave Jenny a moment to figure a clever way to trick him and Kyle.

She tried to memorize the turns they made, but there were too many. Soon they were taking a ramp entrance to a tollway, and Jenny grew less confident of whether they were headed east, west, north, or south.

She spent some time trying to figure out if these guys were part of the TriTopTechRun Game competition or were with the ShrinkWithers. She decided they were part of the game competition because they were careful not to hurt her. Based on information she had been given in the last games, an evil group known as the ShrinkWithers, aimed for total domination of Earth. They aimed for complete destruction of Earth's vegetation and mineral resources for short-term gain, and disregard for any people not in the ShrinkWithers' inner circle. They would not have been reasonable if they caught her.

5

Pick Yourself Up

Stale. Damp. Cold. Moldy.

The ground moved with tiny cave life. Was that a spider crawling across her foot? Meg's senses registered the smells and sounds of her unfamiliar surroundings before her eyes opened to reveal a shadowy underground cavern. She heard water trickling over on her left, maybe ten feet away. The tantalizing thought of a cool drink sliding down her desert-dry throat was more than she could bear at the moment. She distracted herself by focusing on the cold ground beneath her face and started a mental countdown, checking on her body parts.

Right cheekbone flattened into the rough dirt surface. Hearing muffled. Sore spot on my shoulder.

Yes, really sore shoulder. Feet and wrists bound tight. No wiggle room.

Meg turned her head, allowing her ear to unfold from its unnatural angle. She spat out some gritty dirt. She had no clue how much time had passed since she was put there, but based on the dim light coming from the opening to the cave, she estimated it was about seven o'clock p.m. on the day of their capture.

Meg was careful not to move or make any noise so she wouldn't attract attention, in case whoever had thrown her in there was close by.

Patience was the hardest part to manage in a situation like this. Meg needed to assess her condition, her location, and possible escape chances. Denying herself the luxury of a gigantic scream for help, Meg lifted her head when she heard a slight scraping sound. It stopped. She lay still and counted to ten. Nothing. No other noises.

Meg continued her body-part checklist. Everything ached from her head to her toes, as if she had run a double marathon. Her right shoulder had shooting pains every so often, going from her neck down to her upper arm. It was likely it had been bashed when she was thrown or dropped onto the ground. There was a lot of pain, yet her shoulder had no bones out of place.

Her ankles were lashed to each other tightly, as were her hands. The binding material felt like leather strapping, allowing no movement. Her thoughts were interrupted by a cough, followed by a loud whisper. *There it goes again. What's that sound?*

"Meg, you there? Is that you, Meg? Answer me! I've been calling you for several minutes. I can't shout, or someone might hear me. Please, Meg, please wake up! Let me know you're okay!"

"Dave? Dave? Where are we? What happened? Stuff hurts. Either I've been sleeping or I've been knocked out for a while. What about you?"

"I'm sore and thirsty, but nothing seems broken or bleeding. I think we've been down here about an hour. Pretty sure I passed out. I've been trying to wake you up most of that time. I'm worried about Jenny. They must have her by now. I heard them say their other crew was going over to get her after we were safely on the road. Do you think they'll bring her here?"

"I know we both think she'll be able to take care of herself, but things seem to get worse each year, and one day I fear her skills may fail her and . . ."

Meg always tried to be as strong as Dave and Jenny, but these captures upset her. She wasn't always able to hide her nerves. Meg knew that building their skills to tackle the ShrinkWithers near their home territory was important, but her common sense feared for their lives.

"Don't say it. Don't even think it! We've been lucky up to now. I need to believe our luck will continue. I can't bear to think what will happen. Not only to our family, but to . . ." Dave's usual keep-it-together attitude sputtered to a halt. He wanted to make Meg feel hopeful, even while he had big doubts.

Meg took advantage of his pause. "I know, but it's getting too crazy, and it's all my fault. I never should've agreed to involve the kids in this. It seemed a great opportunity for all of us to fight the impact on our climate, to keep our planet healthy and our resources flowing, but it gets more dangerous each time. If we succeed, everything we learn can be shared with others, but I should've resisted. I shouldn't have agreed with you. I know the purpose of these games is to prepare well-trained groups to infiltrate the ShrinkWithers' compound and headquarters, but my fears are overtaking my confidence."

Dave, feeling himself sliding into Meg's doubtful mood, responded, "Yes, it made good sense to both of us in the beginning, but Jen and Branch deserve choices and lives of their own. Not many parents volunteer to expose their kids to danger like this. This is more than we bargained for. Something is different. This can't just be TriTech we're battling in here."

"I know, Dave. It seems—"

At that moment, the makeshift wooden slat door covering the cave flew open. Branch came flying in at a dead run, all out of breath, shouting, "Let's go! Gotta get outta here fast! They're after me, only about five minutes behind. Get up! Follow me! I've got a plan. Only one way out of here. We go now or we won't be able to escape at all!"

Branch looked like your typical ten-year-old camper in khaki shorts, rumpled red T-shirt, worn sneakers, and a baseball hat with the brim backward. His backpack sagged low from its weight, but it didn't seem to be slowing him down.

"Branch, it's so good to see you! Who captured you from home last night? We were petrified you'd been grabbed by the ShrinkWithers when you disappeared. Keeping Jenny from getting suspicious was almost impossible. We didn't want to worry her. She had enough on her plate with the new TriTopTechRun-2 starting this summer. As you can see, it seems to have started earlier than planned."

"Don't worry, Mom. I've still got the lucky plastic baggie you gave me." Branch patted his pants pocket, where he always carried it.

"The AstroSPAN game team picked me up from soccer and told me I couldn't call you guys to tell. They wanted to test us all in emergency circumstances, so they wanted it to be a surprise to you guys and Jenny, and for me to complete a day of power testing before this year's game started. No time for more now."

Branch looked at his mom and dad's restrictive leather binders and blinked six times. Magically, the belts seemed to come to life and snap to attention, splitting open at every bend as they slithered off onto the floor, leaving Meg and Dave wobbly but free. They stood with some effort, stretching their arms and legs to work their circulation, then started off at a slow trot—all they could manage now. Dave noticed his left leg was weak. Something was amiss. He'd been so worried about Meg, he hadn't paid attention to his own injuries. He limped due to a stabbing pain in his thigh.

Meg, Dave, and Branch scrambled up to the cave's narrow opening, toward the light at the end of the shallow tunnel on the side of a sheer hillside, somewhere in a heavily forested area—one brave little boy in the lead, one scared mom with a bruised shoulder and a scratched cheek, and a very worried dad with a syncopated walk. Branch wished he could always summon magic to help them out. He was glad it had worked quickly this time.

They picked their way down the mountainside, moving as fast as their injuries allowed, while the day's light faded. Determination appeared on their faces, but their bodies signaled desperation. They all looked brave on the outside, but each one feared that any minute they would be caught and "Game Over—You Lost!"

6

Dust Yourself Off

"**W**atch the screen on the left," directed a short, neatly dressed man in his late forties. He turned in his chair, a broad smile on his face. "I didn't expect them to get out so quickly, but there they are. I forgot to figure on Branch getting to them that fast. He's something, isn't he? Branch beat our projected time estimates by at least two hours. Where did we mess up?"

Game Guides Ralph, Terrence, and Tony occupied the main TriTopTechRun command post in the west tower of the digital research complex, accessible only to AstroSPAN planners. Security measures were extremely complex; entry passwords and codes were altered every three hours around the clock. While the overall mission of the competitive games they monitored was to combat further global warming and climate change mega-disasters, the Game Guides tried to treat their jobs like a game, to avoid stress overload. Some days it worked, some days it didn't.

"We didn't mess up. They're all a year older and smarter than last time. What did you expect, Ralph? You know the plan, I know the plan, but they have a lot of smarts, and they're tough and creative and . . ." Terrence was ticked that Ralph questioned their skills.

Ralph and Terrence leaned forward in their swivel chairs to observe the actions on the three monitors in front of them. Tony stood behind them, taking notes as they watched. The monitors were trained on Jenny, Mark, and Kyle traveling up the highway. The Guides had a full view of the car and its occupants. One screen captured the front of the car, another the rear, and a middle screen viewed inside the car. All eyes darted back and forth among the three screens.

A gurgling scream came from the car scene in the middle monitor. Jenny squiggled out of her seatbelt, reached forward to the front seat, and grabbed Kyle's throat with her arm wrapping tightly in a strangle hold. Kyle, taken by surprise, was now speechless from her continuing pressure.

Gosh! She's really strong for a twelve-year-old kid was Kyle's last thought as he started to black out.

Mark was startled but could only grab a quick peek at this new problem in the passenger seat beside him and still manage to keep the car on the road at seventy-five miles per hour. He slammed his foot on the brakes and aimed for the shoulder of the road. He hoped he didn't spin out and send them rolling over the drop-off beyond the shoulder of the highway.

We can't control this girl. Why does she think she can ruin my day like this? Why did I take this job, anyway?

Jenny held on even tighter to Kyle's throat as the car hit a deep pothole, bursting a rear tire and disabling their vehicle. She braced herself for a possible crash as they came to a burned-rubber halt on the shoulder of the busy highway.

It took Mark no time at all to throw open his door and scramble around the car, intending to grab Jenny and break her hold on Kyle's throat. Mark thought Kyle didn't look so good in that particular color of pink rising up his face. *Serves him right. He should have been more vigilant. Sometimes I think he just doesn't have a clue. In fact, I know he doesn't, but I keep hoping.*

Jenny clenched her jaw tightly at precisely the moment Mark flung open his driver door. Opening the driver door opened all the door locks. In one quick motion, Jenny released her stronghold on Kyle's neck and bounded out of the car.

She started running up the highway toward oncoming traffic. Her plan was to catch a ride with someone who was driving back the way they had come. She knew she was breaking her mom's rule about rides with strangers, but surely this qualified as the exception. "It's okay, Mom. If you can hear me. I'll be just fine."

"Kyle, get out of the car! Help me catch her. I can't do this alone!"

Mark was furious with Kyle for letting his guard down, but he was even more disgusted with himself for being so easily tricked by Jenny. She was already a half block ahead of them, running on the side of the road, waving her arms for help. Mark was desperate to catch her. He was torn between being angry at her escape and scared she'd be injured running up the highway.

He heard the car door slam as Kyle jumped out. Kyle was still groggy from the stranglehold.

They both loped down the road, running as fast as two guys who sit most of their work days can run. No way would they be able to beat a kid like Jenny, but they needed to try.

Just then, there was a terrible screech of tires as a camouflage-colored Jeep pulled to a sudden stop alongside Jenny. A brawny arm reached out and scooped Jenny into the Jeep. Mark's fears of mission failure had come true so, of course, he immediately did the most logical thing. He stopped to spin around to face Kyle and blame everything on him as the Jeep careened down the highway with Jenny inside.

"Kyle, you potato-head! You're an absolute no-good-for-nothing creep! This mess is your fault! You didn't take this seriously from the beginning.

You thought this job would be a snap. 'How can getting a little girl-kid be hard?' you said. Well, now you know, and we're both going to be demoted and knocked down the work ladder—back to driving packages back and forth like pizza delivery boys! Whaddya say to that, Mr. Four-Cheese-Crispy-Crust-Hot-Pizza Guy?!"

Mark felt good unloading his anxiety on Kyle. He believed Kyle never worked hard enough and didn't hold up his end of their load. He believed this loss was Kyle's fault.

* * *

The three AstroSPAN Guides back in the tower were trying hard to keep straight faces as they watched this scene play out on the monitor.

Ralph broke the strained silence in the room with a loud laugh, which created two more explosive laughs from Terrence and Tony, once they decided it was useless to pretend this was anything but ridiculous.

Terrence stopped laughing and spoke first. He had a worried look on his face, something they'd never seen before. He always wore his quiet authority with confidence. Terrence never let anyone see a crack in that confidence.

"Take a minute to think this through. This isn't funny! Did anyone get the Jeep's license plate number? Guess what, guys. That's not our Jeep!"

That did it. That stopped the belly laughs really fast.

"What are you saying?" Tony asked.

"I'm telling you, those aren't our people. Somebody's got Jenny, and it's not us. We've lost control. Someone *not* in our game is in our game!" Terrence was near panic level now. Tony and Ralph finally realized something was very wrong.

"Who the heck are they?" said Ralph. "What's going on? What can we do from here?"

Terrence got very quiet. He took a deep breath in, let it out slowly, and stuck both hands in his pockets, saying each word deliberately, as if he were talking to children.

"Let's. Keep. Calm. We. Must. Stay. Focused."

Tony and Ralph waited for him to spout one of his brilliant ideas. They waited. A minute went by. No brilliance.

Finally, Terrence picked up his cell phone. Before he dialed, he said, "Sorry, boys, I never thought there would come a day when I haven't a clue what to do next. Time for me to call in the big guys."

Tony exploded, "Big guys? We *are* the big guys! We've directed this from the beginning. We started it. We selected all the players. We solved all the problems. Everyone has always lived happily ever after. We get paid the big bucks. Who else is there?"

7

Start All Over Again

Coming around a sudden curve in the path, Meg narrowly avoided a huge rock as she neared the bottom of the ravine in her frantic run down the hill. She swerved, then stopped abruptly, thinking she heard Jenny whisper something in her earpiece. Throwing up her hand to gesture a halt, she shushed Dave as he overtook her. She was certain she'd heard Jenny say something. It sounded like, "I'll be fine."

The crackle of the small underbrush branches breaking under her feet as she and Dave ran down the hill had blocked out the rest. She listened for more. Nothing.

Meg was sure it was Jenny's voice she had heard, and she had sounded okay. She grabbed Dave's hand, and together they dashed to the bottom, following Branch's lead. Their breath came in swift pants as they caught up to him. Branch showed no sign of being winded at all. Dave and Meg had to stop running to recover their energy.

"Wait a minute, guys. I'm out of steam," said Dave.

"We can't afford that minute. Let's get to the safe house before we lose track of the path. It's getting dark really fast now."

"How far out do you think we are, Meg?" Dave tried to sound calm.

"Well, we ended up closer than I thought because we angled our way down the mountain, so I guess we're a little under a half mile. Can you make it?" Meg winced, almost caving in to her shoulder pain. She wasn't certain they were actually that close, but she believed it best to pretend at this point.

"Yup. My leg has exactly four blocks worth of vim and vigor in it, so let's go."

Dave was fibbing underneath his reassuring smile. He didn't fool Meg one bit. They both knew there was no choice but to keep going. Each one was keeping a stiff upper lip, trying to stay positive for the sake of the other.

Hugging the line of tall red pine trees near the edge of the valley, they avoided the open grassy area so their movement couldn't be seen. Their instinct from last year's games served them well, even though they were in a different location. The previous game had been under less challenging circumstances. Their children had never been put in danger; there were far more smiles, no injuries, no kidnappings, and many safety stations with time-out breaks.

Something was different this year.

Dave stayed about fifty feet behind Meg so he wouldn't be tempted to talk to her. That was the hardest part. They were used to sharing everything. Now, silence was a necessity. They did not feel safe. They did not know who was observing them, or why. It made sense to avoid being seen.

Branch wound his way down the narrow tree-covered path, taking care to stay well ahead of his mom and dad yet close enough so they could see him and make no wrong turns. The path wasn't really a path. He was picking his way through tight, low bushes, which grabbed at his legs while he ran. Branch knew he needed to stay separate from his parents, to avoid attracting attention. He always felt they were being watched. Plus, the technology for this game was sure to be more advanced than the last time—more gadgets, new powers, greater magic. Learning how to use it all was managed in actual practice, but Branch longed for some user manuals. He loved reading user guides.

As much as he wanted to lean on his parents, he knew they depended on him for getting them to safety now that each had an injury. There were never any injuries the other time. He couldn't suppress one nagging thought. *It's not a game this time. It can't be a game. I'm not having any fun.*

And then he knew.

Right! It's not a game. These guys are for real. I've got to tell Jen.

8

Keep It To Yourself

*F*ine! *Just fine! Peachy keen. My gramma always says that when something goes wrong. Who are these people?* Jenny had never been so surprised. Someone had grabbed her off the road and flung her into a green-and-khaki camouflage Jeep. Snatched from her fabulous escape, just as she was thinking she had so cleverly outwitted Mark and Kyle. She was pretty sure Mark and Kyle were part of the TriTop game team, sent to provide challenges to be mastered, to prepare for eventual real disasters. She sensed that the woman next to her was *not* part of the game.

Jenny had landed with a bounce on the back seat, squished up tight next to someone twice her size, and sneaked a look sideways, viewing the woman's muscular arms bulging out of her short sleeves.

She is definitely a workout wonder, like Mom always says whenever she sees someone in good shape. Jen suppressed an urge to scream. *When in doubt, close eyes and think. Mustn't look scared.*

Urgent whispers crackled through her tech-dot earpiece implanted behind her left earlobe. She could barely understand the words.

"Jen, please . . . If you hear me, give two quick sneezes . . . Need to tell . . ."

Thrilled at hearing Branch's voice for the first time since this adventure began, Jenny immediately calmed down. *Branch is safe! He's alive!* She regained her nerve and made two *sneeze sounds*, separated by three seconds of silence in between. *Branch sounded very grown-up just now. That's odd— not at all like my little kid brother.*

Delighted to hear Jen's sneezes, Branch wanted to talk to her, to find out if she was okay. Not possible now. He had only a few seconds. His muffled whisper came out in brief spurts, like he was running and panting.

"Jen, this is real. Repeat . . . This is real! We are Go! Pull out all your powers. You must . . ."

Branch's voice trailed off. Jenny stifled her need to blurt out, "What was the last part?" She didn't want the woman next to her to know she could communicate with someone.

What must she do? Panic shivers crawled up her arms and took hold of her brain as she registered

48

Branch's word "real." *What does he mean?* And then she understood. *This is the real thing! We aren't playing a game!*

No. That's not possible. We were always told the practice games will go on for several more years until I'm an adult and I test all my powers and they work.

As she struggled to put all her thoughts together, she realized a new shock. *Surprise! Surprise! Branch is a part of it this time. Oh my gosh! Branch is a part of it this time. He was always too little before. When and where did he get training?*

Jenny shrank down in her seat, trying to become invisible, but of course that was silly. *Kidnapped! Again!*

She glanced at the tough gal next to her. She averted her eyes quickly, before Muscle Girl could notice she was looking at her. The woman wore a brown-and-black jumpsuit, like a uniform, with many pockets—all of which bulged. *With weapons,* Jen figured.

She checked the driver. She could see only the back of his head. He had dark-brown hair, shaggy to the shoulder, topped with a Chicago Blackhawks hockey cap. She thought she noticed a tiny tattoo on the right side of his neck, peeking out from under the cap. He kept adjusting the cap, pushing it down over that side. Once, when he sneezed, his cap flipped forward briefly and she saw the tattoo: a capital S and a capital W. He took the curves on two wheels. No one talked. No radio music.

Jenny's observation training kicked in as she

surveyed her surroundings. She wasn't sure which direction they were headed, just that the trees were getting much closer together. There were few cars passing them from the oncoming lane. She tried to note buildings or landmarks, but saw none. Just forest. Forest all around. They were getting so deep into the woods, it was hard to tell time. Gigantic trees blocked the sun.

"Who are you? Where are you taking me? I have good friends tracking my every move. They won't be happy you took me. You have ten minutes to let me go, or you'll be destroyed," Jenny said, her words calm but her heart racing. She waited for an answer. There was none. Neither the driver nor Jumpsuit Wonder Woman offered an answer. They just stared at the road ahead. Jenny could sense their eyes glancing at her once in a while, though their heads didn't swivel at all.

Branch told me to pull out all my powers. This might be the exact right time to try it. Sometimes it works. Sometimes it doesn't. Here goes.

Jenny closed her eyes, pictured her favorite place, imagined her brother next to her, took a long breath, counted to seven silently, and waited.

"Where is she? How could you let her go?" the driver shouted at Jumpsuit Gal.

"Are you crazy? I didn't let her go. I'm sitting here minding my business. Got my eyes real close on her. One minute she's here. Next minute she's gone. Completely gone!"

"That's not possible. I've got the K-Packtor

right here in my pocket. We were told if we had that thing turned on, she couldn't disappear. This is impossible! We're sunk. This isn't what's supposed to happen. We've lost our catch!"

* * *

In an instant, Jenny found herself out of the car, standing in the middle of an enormous bank of trees, at the bottom of a hill several hundred feet high. She twirled to check on all directions. Only one problem. No brother.

This isn't the way it's supposed to work. I'm supposed to land exactly in my vision. I pictured Branch, just like I'm supposed to. I should've landed right next to him, wherever he is. What am I doing wrong?

9

Whew,
That Was Close

As he neared the base of the mountain, avoiding the low northern white pine tree limbs intent on ripping his face and arms, Branch kept trying to reach Jenny on his transponder earpiece. No luck. He could only hope she had received his complete message, telling her this time the game was real. Their connection had sounded open for a moment, but no words from Jenny. Branch at least had heard background static, so he had hope. That spindly thread of hope was the only thing that held him together. His thoughts spilled over with dozens of questions. What would he tell Jen, now that it seemed they were involved in both a game competition and a possible ShrinkWither takeover? How could they tell the difference in each situation? How would they know who was in charge? Things were happening so fast.

"Jen, are you there? Can you hear me?" Branch tried again, desperate to hear Jenny's voice.

Nothing. Not even static this time.

Branch tried not to panic. He was about a hundred yards ahead of his parents when he slowed down, darted behind one of the larger pines, and signaled back to them to stay still. Mom motioned to Dad, and their strange wilderness marathon came to a halt. Branch was thankful for this pause. As he took cover, he listened for any sounds of followers. He was still careful to keep separate while they were moving and when they stopped, so they could all stay hidden. He was glad to stop now and think about the past year.

One year ago, Branch had been both excited and scared in the first TriTopTechRun Games competition. It was the first time he was involved, the first time he was away from home by himself. The tech gadgets thrilled him. They reminded him of AlphaWaver, which he loved playing on the computer at home. And in the TriTopTechRun Game, whenever he designed the structures on the monitor screen they came to life out on the tarmac, tucked deep inside a secluded forest. Abracadabra! Magic arise!

Remembering his past computer successes and last year's TechRun competition cheered him up during this break in the action. *This is just like the game. I've got this. I can survive. I can win. I've done it before. I can do it again.*

In the game competitions, first Branch had imagined a creative design. Next, he spent a few hours coding it into the computer. His fantastic castles and moats and turrets and drawbridges had appeared just up the road, outside the building where he and the Game Guides worked. Then the AstroSPAN researchers ran through technical strategy lessons, along with strength training in actual life and real time the following week, according to complex game formulas set up. His little boy's dreams had come to life!

He remembered Jenny hadn't been happy when he returned home after last year's game and told her he had designed that layout. He tried to swear her to secrecy because the Guides told him he couldn't tell anyone, not even his family. He wasn't sure he could trust Jen not to tell Mom and Dad. He and Jen always told Mom and Dad everything. Now he was told he *wasn't* to tell anybody. He always trusted Jen, but he had doubts now. Not because she wasn't trustworthy, but because he didn't trust the AstroSPAN Guides. He worried that maybe they had super mind-reading talents which would cause him trouble for betraying their trust.

Jenny thought he had made it all up. She hadn't believed him at all!

She had shouted at him with her angry

cheeks-puffed-out face, warning him he was telling a preposterous lie. She was certain AstroSPAN would send him back home if they ever found out he lied. Even though he hated that Jenny didn't believe him, he could tell by her clenched teeth and urgent tone that it was best to stay quiet. So, he did.

That was the first time in his life Jenny had not believed him. Up to that point, he could always count on her to defend him whenever their parents thought he wasn't telling the truth. He usually told the truth, but he had a wonderful imagination. Sometimes it took over his story. It was hard to tell where truth ended and Branch-fiction began.

Why didn't she believe me that day?

His favorite memory was that he had played such an important part in that game. No one— not his parents, not the other players, not even his sister Jenny—knew he was the chief guy behind the design. He had earned that position by beating a bunch of players in the TechManTrials computer tryout. They had pulled him out of line at the end of a long practice round. He thought he was in trouble for doing something wrong, but the Magistrate told him he had amazing promise in game design. And that's how he earned his CreateChief title.

Branch chuckled, remembering that his parents and Jenny had thought he was safe at home with his fun babysitting aunt while they were training. Little did they know. *It had been so hard keeping that secret.*

A slight tremor in the ground shocked Branch out of his memories. It grew to a rumble. He collapsed flat and face down, protecting his head and chest, as they had taught him. There wasn't a bush or anything nearby he could grab, just a large dead tree stump he ducked behind, surrounded by grasses. Branch felt he was going to whirl up into the air. Mom and Dad were somewhere behind him. He hoped they had noticed where he was, in case . . .

Certain that the shaking was an earthquake, Branch thought it was best to stay glued to the ground, away from a tree or anything that could topple. But he feared to expose himself out in the open. He felt a strong wind gust on his right and turned his face to look.

A huge helicopter was about to land, less than a hundred feet away. His first thought was to get up and run toward it, screaming for help. Then he remembered his training and stayed down. As the rotors slowed, the chopper hovered, almost silent as it descended and set its runners down. Funny how quiet it was now, when just one moment before the landscape had trembled.

Somewhat hidden by four-foot-tall grasses, Branch rubbed his face back and forth into the musty earth to camouflage himself before turning toward the helicopter again. He kept his mouth shut to avoid swallowing the dirt. Three figures stood in the helicopter's open doorway, preparing to jump. All three wore tight black spandex bodysuits.

Jet-black masks with tiny eye slits covered their faces completely. They looked like sleek ninjas.

They hurtled out of the copter when it was about eight feet off the ground. On landing, they scattered in three different directions, Middle Ninja heading straight for Branch.

Branch assessed how far he was from safe cover. There was none. He was now fully exposed. The helicopter rotors had swept the underbrush clear. Now it was at least fifty yards to the edge of the trees. No buildings. No shacks. No barns. He reached into his pocket, clutched the remote Brain-Mason controller, quickly texted "Pyramid Rise," and hit Send.

Faster than he expected, a huge earthen pyramid structure expanded upward from the dirt area between his position and Middle Ninja, rising at a rate of fifty feet per second. Branch grabbed onto a secure protruding rock to stop his body from going any higher as he catapulted up one side of the rising pyramid. He halted about a hundred feet up, on the opposite side from the ninjas, out of their sight. He caught a brief glimpse of Middle Ninja spinning wildly down the pyramid's opposite face as it grew higher and higher. He hoped Mom and Dad were okay and still hidden. He had no idea where Tall Ninja and Short Ninja were.

He didn't have to wait long to find out. He turned to look down and saw both ninjas dangling by long wires reaching from their belts up to the helicopter. How they had become attached was a mystery. The helicopter was swinging them in long arcs, aiming right for him. Branch grabbed the Brain-Mason remote from his pocket and without thinking twice about any consequences typed in "Release Lions." Until now, he had only created buildings and structures. He had designed no living beings in any of his practice game training, so he wasn't sure they were even a possibility. No one had talked about creating human or animal helpers, but today's situation could benefit from a try.

He hit Send and waited for magic. Or a miracle. Or technology.

Fearing disaster when he clicked Send, Branch shut his eyes for a moment but opened them to see Tall Ninja and Short Ninja tumbling into a gigantic moat that surrounded the pyramid as it grew higher and higher, heading toward the sun. Middle Ninja was nowhere to be seen.

The last thing Branch remembered of the event was the roar of several lions, thrashing in the murky green water in the moat.

10

Game Day

Jenny stomped her feet to release her frustration. She couldn't believe she hadn't landed by Branch after her brain-thought teleported her out of danger and away from her second kidnapping. She was concerned that daylight was disappearing as she reached the end of her first day of involvement in what appeared to be the game competition.

She checked the tree-covered area around her and decided to dash for dense vegetation while trying to reach Branch on the transponder. She barreled along toward the thickest low branches off to the east, coming to a breathless stop twenty feet into the underbrush—sliding on slippery leaves, losing her balance, and landing on her right hip. She reached to touch her earpiece to contact

Branch but could not feel it in place.

Jenny panicked at the thought of losing contact with Branch. She stood up, careful not to disturb anything.

Jenny bent down while she sifted through the leaves looking for her transponder, relieved to see its blinking edge near where she had landed. Since it was almost dark now, she would never have found it without its glow. Her trainer had told her if it ever dropped out, its shiny silver-blue glow would activate but be visible only to someone on her team. It worked perfectly! She picked it up, blew the dirt off, and replaced it in the little depression under a skin flap behind her left ear. That flap had been sewn on without a seam showing during the last games.

How clever that the ear tech-dot is the size of a tiny mole, she thought. Jenny knew it was invisible when back in place properly. She decided to avoid trying to communicate with Branch before she could figure out her exact location. She knew he was probably beyond frantic by this time, not knowing where she was, scared of his wimpy little kid shadow—lost without Mom and Dad and her.

How is he going to survive in the real world?

"Jen! Jen, where are you?" Branch's voice was raspy, but it came through the earpiece loud and clear.

He had run down the pyramid like a gazelle—to escape the helicopter ninjas and lunging lions in the moat—as fast as a ten-year-old soccer player could go. When he reached a large concrete structure that appeared magically halfway down the hill, he sped inside and became engulfed in swaying blue, purple, and red laser lights, with a bit of pink thrown in. When he adjusted his earpiece, Branch noticed he couldn't see his hand or his arm. He looked down. His legs and torso had disappeared as well. The lights had made him invisible. *Perfect!*

"*Thank heavens!*" Jenny had heard him calling to her, and she answered with great relief. "Branch, I landed somewhere inside a vast forest. Trees, lots of trees. Not sure where I am. I was captured a second time, and I had to use my tele-thought to escape, but it stuck me somewhere wrong. I used the right words. I know I did. I should be right next to you, but I'm not. And it's dark now!"

"Okay, Jen, think through this. Calm down. Give me a minute."

Jenny wanted to explode with laughter. *Is that really my little brother telling ME to calm down? When did we reverse roles? I'm the heroine of these adventures. He's just my little brother, who stays home and waits for us to return. I'm bigger and stronger and smarter.*

I'm the peacock. He's the sparrow! Doesn't he know that? What's going on here? Jenny felt herself getting hysterical, then calm, swinging back and forth between laughter and fear. Nothing made any sense. She was exhausted from her rough day.

Worst of all, and feeling very strange, Jenny relaxed as Branch took over leading. What was happening seemed odd but helped her feel safer at the same time.

"Okay, Jen, I've got it! Just remembered, last time I designed the game—"

That's it! This has gone far enough. Someone is playing tricks on me!

Jenny cut off Branch sharply, mid-sentence. "What are you talking about? *You* designed the game? What do you mean *you*? This is the first time we've been together in this. Branch, I need you to make sense right now. We're in a big mess here. We don't have time for your childish fantasy. I need you to focus. Just focus, for once. Please. This isn't a game!"

Branch knew they didn't have time to go into his entire story. They had to get going. He could feel disaster gaining ground on them. His confession would have to wait, and Jen would have to swallow her pride and blindly trust his judgment.

"I'll explain later, Jen. Trust me."

Branch reached deep inside his brain, trying to remember the words that would help them out. He'd been told to use them only in a desperate situation, after he tried all other solutions. He knew he didn't exactly have time for testing other solutions. Branch needed a big win, and he needed it now!

He squeezed his eyes tightly shut, crouched down, and spun around six times at near wonder-warp speed while picturing Jenny with her sunny, smiling face standing in the middle of a forest. He came to a sudden halt, dizzy but upright, and shouted,

Crunch-a-bunch
Creepy-weepy
Alabaster Marble-Master
Gondola Garble-Trickster
Sing-song

Branch wished that when he opened his eyes he would see the chant had worked. He opened his eyes. Nothing had happened.

He reviewed his words quickly. They had to work. They were all he had. All he had to save them. Then he remembered.

Of course! He'd left out the master keyword: Galahad. Checking his surroundings once more for anything moving, he crouched down again. He spun around exactly six times, definitely at near warp speed. He saw Jenny's smart and smiling face in his mind's eye. Halting suddenly to say the chant one more time, this time with all of its words, Branch spit out the chant with force.

Crunch-a-bunch
Creepy-weepy
Alabaster Marble-Master
Gondola Garble-Trickster
GALAHAD Sing-song!

At precisely the moment Branch completed the last line, he and Jenny found themselves together, leisurely swimming side by side, matching stroke for stroke. They were inside what appeared to be a gigantic plastic bubble filled with warm water, floating through the air a couple of miles above the ground. The water was warm and matched the color of the sky. They had both been in total darkness before; now they were in full sun, inside a perfect sphere bubble. Though they were high above the ground and completely enclosed, they could feel a soft breeze each time they surfaced, which wasn't frequently. Strange! It felt like they had been underwater for at least fifteen minutes. Wow! Without breathing. Needing no air at all!

Peculiar, Jenny thought. *What is happening?* In the back of her brain, Jenny felt like there was something she must talk about with Branch. She just couldn't remember what it was. All she could think of was something her mom always said when she couldn't remember: *For the life of me . . .*

Branch turned around at the end of their thirteenth or fourteenth swim lap and started to say something to Jenny, but the right words escaped him. He figured they'd come back soon. He just kept swimming.

It . . . was . . . so . . . very . . . r . . . e . . . l . . . a . . . x . . . i . . . n . . . g.

Branch and Jenny soon forgot everything that had happened to them that day. They continued to swim, getting more and more relaxed, serious thoughts escaping them.

Stroke. Glide. Stroke. Glide.

With every glide, Branch's thoughts cleared and his body relaxed further. Before long, he felt as though all they'd ever done was swim like this together. Forever.

11

Daddy-Doubt

Having lost sight of Branch, who was too far ahead of them, Meg and Dave scrambled to the bottom of the ravine on their own. No longer able to walk far, and not wanting to shout, Dave made a clumsy dive at Meg, pulled her to the ground with him, and motioned to be quiet. He whispered a weak, "Stop walking. Danger. Avoid open area."

Dave no longer wanted to maintain a safe distance from Meg to avoid attracting attention. He was reaching a point where he didn't care if they were caught. He was exhausted. Feeling like he was going to pass out soon, Dave didn't want to risk losing sight of her. The game no longer mattered. It was getting way too rough. He didn't remember ever feeling so helpless in the past competitions. There seemed to be a huge magnetic pull on his muscles, especially in his legs. He let out a tremendous groan, something he had never done in the presence of Meg and the kids. It showed defeat, and he never wanted to convey that attitude to the family he loved so much. After all, he was a dad, and he took his dad-job seriously.

Meg also was trying not to show how weak she had become in the past several hours. Every muscle in her body screamed for rest. She saw Dave was fading fast. Meg nodded that she understood. They would stop for a while, thankful for the cover of the dense bushes and saplings that grew around the fallen tree trunks, deep in the wooded area. Even though it was still afternoon, they saw no blue sky in the treetop openings above their heads. They were more protected in the tight vegetation of this comfy forest cocoon if they stayed off major roads and open trails. Meg rolled over gently to change positions to keep her muscles loose.

Neither spoke while they gulped in some much-needed air. Finally, Meg whispered, "I've never seen you so worried, Dave. I know your leg hurts, but there's more, isn't there? You aren't talking us through like you always do. What's wrong?"

Dave blurted his response. "I'm wondering why I ever said yes to getting my family involved in these ridiculous games in the first place!"

There, he'd said it. He couldn't believe it had taken him this long to share his doubts with Meg.

Now he was certain he'd been wrong to agree to involve his family in the attempt to prevent a global disaster. The plan he helped create on paper wasn't working well in actual practice.

"Dave, things are hard for all families now. Remember when you first signed us up for helping? You talked it over with me. We both agreed, don't forget. It's not all on you."

Dave tried to reassure Meg. "Yes, but only if we could stay together as a family and the kids would be safe. I'm not at all sure we made the right decision—"

Meg cut him off before he could break down completely, beaten by his daddy-doubt. "Enough! Don't think so hard! Either you believe in us, or you don't. We will not fail. Evil will not defeat us. We will experience nothing we can't fix!" Meg hoped she sounded convincing enough to shake Dave off his doomsday thinking. She felt so unsettled seeing him like this.

Dave wanted to stand, to emphasize his strength for their next step. But he could manage only to lift himself up on his elbows. His thighs burned with pain.

He found it hard to admit he was losing his belief in their ability. It felt good to hear Meg show strength in her words. He let a tiny slip of a smile slide up one corner of his mouth as Meg took the lead now. He was out of steam. They had always been a wonderful team. When one was down, the other picked up and shouldered the burden, whether the load was mental or physical. He leaned back against the thick tree trunk and closed his eyes.

Meg watched him relax. She sat back and folded her arms around her knees to take a break, waiting for a brilliant idea to hit her. *Any* idea right now would be welcome, even an average one. The underbrush was soft under her legs, the pine trees gave off their healing aromas, and Meg breathed in deeply, feeling a moment of peace.

* * *

Back at AstroSPAN, Guides Tony, Ralph, and Terrence watched the viewing screens closely as Meg and Dave took their break from the action. Ralph noted the difference in their behaviors. Dave seemed defeated. Meg sounded willing to take charge. Her stamina clearly surpassed Dave's at this point. Odd. Dave was a champion, in every way. At least he had always demonstrated that in all their tests and practice sessions. Something was going on here that Ralph couldn't explain.

Ralph decided to ask the others if they saw what he saw. Part of him wanted them to see it as well. Part of him wanted them to tell him he needed new glasses or a new brain—that his thinking was wrong. Ralph decided this was the time to ask them.

"There, do you see it?"

Tony answered first. "Yeah, Ralph, I'm lookin' at 'em. Not much to see. They've passed out. I say we take a break here. The next phase is going to be really rough, and we won't be able to take our eyes off the screen for a long time."

"There. There it is again."

"What, Ralph? Whatcha talkin' about?"

"Meg. Look at Meg! There, right there!" Ralph shouted, pointing to the bottom of the screen where Meg's knees had been just a minute before. Her legs, from the knees down, were missing.

12

Sparrow Flies

Branch woke up first. His eyes were open. His brain was shut. He was surrounded by water, completely submerged. He felt his body fold up. He needed something quick. What was it?

Air. Need air! Can't breathe!

His brain snapped awake. Panic set in. He jerked his knees straight down into the water, opening his legs out straight. He flung his hands above his head, forming a perfect arrow, reaching for the surface of the water. Branch took three dolphin kicks, broke through the surface, and coughed hard to get the water out of his throat and lungs. He remembered they were in a gigantic sealed bubble, about the size of thirty hot air balloons. He stuck his head back under the water to watch Jenny, who appeared to be still asleep. Asleep while swimming. Without taking any breaths. She looked unconscious, but her arms and legs were moving in rhythmic strokes, alternating between freestyle and breast-strokes. She'd swim along doing one stroke; then she'd switch to the other, smooth as silk. Her face was calm. She wasn't awake.

Jenny looked okay, so Branch took another minute to recover his full senses and figure what to do next. He started swimming above Jenny, observing her and realizing he must have been swimming just like her—underwater, not needing a steady supply of air. Not conscious, but alive. Time had passed. Minutes? Hours? Days? They didn't come up for air, yet they had not drowned. This was beyond odd. Their bubble seemed to move at warp speed over large expanses of trees. When he looked down, Branch could make out a few land objects whizzing by, but they were going so fast, he couldn't identify them.

Suddenly, something larger came into view. It looked like a huge body of water with a gigantic falls at one end. It triggered his memory of a family trip they had made to Niagara Falls when he was about four. *Maybe we're over Niagara. But if we're over Niagara Falls, why don't I hear anything?* Branch had a clear memory of putting his hands over his ears the year they visited—the sound was so loud it frightened him. Perhaps they were too high up in the bubble to hear. Now he heard only the silence in the atmosphere as they passed over land. Peaceful, but eerie.

He could feel himself getting anxious. Blood rushed through his feet and hands, which had been pins-and-needles numb when he first woke up. He had experienced a sensation of icy-cold running up and down his legs and arms. Now his body had heated up to the temperature of a warm tub bath. The water in the bubble was pleasant. Very relaxing. He treaded water to stay afloat while he thought about their options.

His mind flew back to Jen. Just when he figured he had to do something immediately to get Jen awake, she surfaced. Her eyes popped open, and she let out a curdling torrent of words.

"Branch! Where are we? What happened? How long have I been underwater? Why didn't I suffocate? This is crazy!"

Water sputtered from her mouth in a rush as she coughed to clear her throat. She looked like their backyard hose gushing water at their rose bushes on a hot summer day. She had flipped onto her back, turning her head from side to side as she struggled to breathe and make sense of her surroundings. Branch understood exactly what she was going through.

Jenny's quick questions unnerved Branch. He wasn't used to seeing her so agitated. She seemed panicked. He remained calm, hoping that would help keep them both positive and balanced. He gave Jenny his best smile—the one he used when asking for thirds after a huge Thanksgiving dinner, even though he knew the answer would probably be no.

"Glad you're awake, Jen. I think they transported us to this fantastic flying bubble. Must have been put to sleep right after we got here. I don't have any idea exactly where we are, but I think we may have passed over Niagara Falls, or some falls that looked just like it. No idea why we didn't drown while we were swimming, asleep in this transparent bubble. No idea how long we've been unconscious."

Branch worried his nerves were showing. Perhaps he was scaring Jen by listing all those things he had no idea about. But when Jen answered, her voice sounded much more like her usual take-charge, find-a-solution tone.

"Who's pulling our strings? Do you suppose we're under the control of our AstroSPAN guys or the ShrinkWithers? Either way, we've got to get back on the ground somehow. My guess is we're being held up here to keep us away from danger. But we need to get back to help Mom and Dad. They're losing energy, Dad's injury is slowing him down, and I think we're their sole hope."

Jen said this as calmly as possible so Branch wouldn't be too scared, but she had a hard time keeping her fears from overwhelming her, too. She was sure Branch would soon notice how frightened she was. It was difficult to keep her voice steady.

Branch, lost in his own thoughts, didn't appear to notice Jen's hesitation.

"Give me a minute to think, Jen. Quiet for a sec. Let's try to slow us down and figure a way to guide our bubble safely to the ground. Let's look for a soft area to land."

This will not be easy. I hope Jen can come up with something I can have faith in—enough faith for both of us. Maybe we won't be so lucky this time. Maybe I can't hold things together any longer. Branch turned his face away from Jen so his fear wouldn't show.

Jenny's combination of scientific knowledge and magical manipulation had always worked well in the past to get her out of some very dangerous circumstances, but this sphere-in-the-atmosphere trip was testing her nerves and physical skills.

"Branch, I'm really frightened. I've always been *on* the ground before—not *above* it! I feel totally out of control."

"Chill out, Jen! We got up here somehow, and even though we were put to sleep, we're still alive. We can talk and think and move, right? If anything really awful were going to happen to us, it would've already, don't you think?"

"I suppose, but this isn't reasonable. We're in trouble up to our ears, in water up to our ears, and way above the ground—above *everyone's* ears!" She sneaked a peek at Branch to see if he was smiling at her joke. He wasn't.

Deep in thought, Branch seemed to ignore Jenny. Then he shouted out, "I've got it! I've got it!"

"Okay, let's have it." Jenny tried to show excitement, but she wasn't feeling it.

"While you were daydreaming over there, I remembered when we first got put in this sphere. Before we became unconscious, I dived to what seemed to be the bottom. There was an area that looked like a drain of some sort, made of a hard rubber material. Water was slowly exiting through it. The major problem will be to remove that drain cover with the pressure of all this water on it and not be injured by the force. I should at least make a dive down there right now and check things out."

Jenny interrupted him with an excited squeal. "Awesome! Go for it! I'll stay up here on top of the water and watch for you."

Jenny always loved solutions that involved quick decisions and fast action, and she was desperate for escape from their confinement in the bubble. It scared her that they might reach Mom and Dad too late. It may already be too late.

Branch wanted to keep Jen hopeful, but he knew he must prepare her in case of a failure.

"Jen, you need to know that I may not make it back up safely. If not, then you stay here. Let's hope whoever is controlling us is deliberately keeping us safe and not planning to harm us. They may just be trying to separate us. We aren't as much of a threat if we're kept separate."

Jen recognized Branch's attempt to keep her calm, so she pretended she was okay and that she believed him. She smiled and then quickly looked down so he wouldn't see the tears tumbling out of her eyes.

"Okay, gonna dive now. Keep floating right where you are. Try to keep your position, so I can surface near you when I come up."

Branch took a huge breath and dived underwater, heading for what he thought would be the bottom of the bubble, pacing his speed to go the distance. He had so many doubts. How deep is the water? Was oxygen going to be supplied somehow, as it must have been while they'd been swimming asleep? Will there really be something at the bottom of the sphere that will help them out of this mess?

Even if all his questions had "No" for an answer, he knew he had to try. *There are no other choices. Giving up isn't an option. Dive!*

13

Peacock Feathers Ruffle

Jenny had hugged Branch tightly and made a heart shape with her fingers to give him a silent good-luck-I-love-you message before he plunged deep under the water. She had great confidence in Branch now. *It's becoming harder to see him as my goofy little brother. He seems so smart and grown-up.* She realized she would have to stop using rude words whenever she thought of Branch. *He's no longer pesky, that's for sure.*

He certainly had made her rethink all her evil thoughts. Sometimes she had wished she were an only child. Now she couldn't imagine life without Branch. *What a wonderful partner. How could I have doubted his worth? Never again will I play that silly game where I blink my eyes three times and hope, when I open them, he'll disappear. I'm so glad I didn't zap him out of existence. Thank heavens my think-magic always failed me when I tried to do him in.*

Jenny wondered why they hadn't discussed if there was anything she could do while waiting for Branch to report back from the depths of the drain. Branch wanted her to stay close to where he dived. *What could it hurt to explore, in case I can find an alternate opening, in case his plan fails?*

Jenny floated on her back, using a tiny flipper motion with her hands to maintain her position in the water.

She started looking at all four quadrants of the clear casing covering their bubble, to see if there was anything that looked like an opening. It was hard to track which section she was on because there was no variation in any part of the sphere. Seamless. Nothing that could be a marker to return to. And outside the sphere was the solid blue sky, no clouds. Below her was the smooth, dark-turquoise water. As best she could, she tried to make two rotations. At least she thought it was twice.

Just as she had completed her second round, she detected something moving outside the bubble, off to the right. It came into view for less than a second. Since the bubble had a spinning movement of its own, she hoped the rotations were fairly regular and the object would come into sight again. She held her position and waited.

There! There it is again! She squinted her eyes, struggling to make the object clear. It came and went so quickly. She waited for a third pass. This time she was ready. She saw the object closer and much larger than at first. *No. It can't be.* It looked like a raft made of tough vinyl. It was the size of a small boat. *How ridiculous. How can a boat navigate through the atmosphere without gravity pulling it down?*

Of course, she wasn't sure, but up to now she had thought their sphere was cruising along high in the atmosphere. Before she could even think of an explanation, she saw a puff of white smoke explode out from the side of the raft. An object hurtled toward the sphere, aiming straight at her body. She knew she had no place to hide before it hit, so she curled tight, hugging her knees to her chest, with her head underwater to let the water absorb the impact.

The force of the first hit blasted Jenny away from that area of the sphere. She spun around and around, like a bowling ball heading for a strike. Something yanked her down into the water and quickly forced her up to the surface. This happened three more times. The energy from a hit sloshed the water violently back and forth. Each time, she gulped enough air for the next downspin so she felt she had some control, but every spin made her dizzy. Dizzy and filled with dread that the next swoop would be beyond her strength to combat.

Make it stop! Branch! Branch, help!

"Jenny Cranston!" The loudest voice she'd ever heard was calling her name. Where had she heard that voice before?

"Jenny Cranston, it's time for you to get out of that bubble and join us back at home base. Follow my directions, do exactly as I tell you, and you will be safe."

"Who are you? Where are you? Where's my brother Branch?"

The voice didn't answer.

Jenny repeated her questions. She shouted to cover her wobbliness. "Who are you? Where are you? Where's my brother Branch?"

"Never mind about me. Do you want help, or are you giving up? Isn't that just like a girl. Giving up when the going gets tough," the voice answered, sounding irritated.

"How do I know I can trust you? Give me a sign. Otherwise, go away. I'll figure this out by myself. You better stay away from me. I have magic powers, and I can damage you. I will. I really will. Don't make me do it!" Jenny hoped her bravado would scare off whoever was threatening her. She had no weapons at her disposal, only her courage and her bluffing.

The voice laughed. First, it was a tiny tee-hee.

Then, it was a silly giggle.

Next, it grew into a giant guffaw.

It ended with a snort!

That snort. That snort could come only from one person. She'd heard that snort at the ends of all his dumb jokes for many years. *What's he done to his voice?*

"Okay, Branch, not funny. First the shot from that impossible, gravity-defying flying raft. Then your gigantic voice. Where are you? I can't see you."

"I'm on the raft."

"That's not true. You can't be on the raft. The raft is an enemy. It just shot huge missiles into the side of the bubble. But it's odd that everything seems in place. The water still surrounds me and nothing has escaped from the bubble."

"I shot the missile, Jen. Actually, it isn't a missile. It's a giant rubber speaker that attaches to anything, I guess. You can aim it at something, select the material of your target and a power speed ranging from 'Mild Irritation' to 'Harm.' I chose 'Irritation' so it wouldn't penetrate the bubble's surface. The first three glanced off, but the fourth one attached, so I could speak through it. As you heard, it makes someone's voice really loud and scary. Plus, I think it can shoot deadly darts at a target. Aren't you glad I skipped the deadly darts part?"

"Sweet, Branch, really sweet. How did you get out of the bubble? What do I do now?"

"Easy. I dived to the bottom, like we planned. There were lots of mechanical levers sticking up from the drain piece. I noticed they were in a pattern, like constellations in the sky. You know, the shapes made by stars, named after characters in Greek mythology. I studied all the lever shapes, then I chose one to see if it could open the bubble to let me escape."

Jenny interrupted. "Speed up! Quit dragging your scientific excursions into this and tell me how to find the right one."

"Aquarius, the Water Bearer, obviously. I wanted the bubble to spill me out, so what better constellation than the water jug?"

"What if you'd gotten it wrong? Weren't you scared?"

"Needed to get out of there, Jen. Had to take a risk. My intuition was right. Of course, I based it on a dab of my usual superior, logical thinking."

"Get me out of here, Branch. Now!"

14

Hawk Swoops

Meg woke up slowly from what she thought was only a brief nap. She glanced at Dave and saw he was still asleep, his face looking relaxed and peaceful. Meg felt much better than the day before. Nothing hurt anymore, which was odd. The pain she'd experienced before she fell asleep was gone. The pain in her lower legs was gone. She looked down and gasped so loudly that it startled Dave and woke him up.

"What? What was that, Meg?"

"Look! Look at my legs. Where are they? I can't see anything from my knees down. My legs are missing!"

Dave checked and was relieved to see they were still connected to her. "Meg, what are you saying? Your legs are there, just like always. I see them. Don't you?"

Why isn't Dave telling me the truth? What's he hiding? "Dave, stop it. Look, just look!"

"I *did* look, Meg. Both your legs are attached to your body. I'm looking at you, and I see both of them. Stand up and stretch. You're just dizzy from your sleep."

Meg gave Dave one of her are-you-out-of-your-mind looks, but he sounded sure, so she thought she had better try to stand. If she fell over, he'd believe something was amiss. It was worth a try.

"Okay, give me a sec."

She drew a deep breath and willed her body to stand. She was astonished when she didn't fall over.

Dave grinned and said, "See? Told ya so."

Meg looked down at her legs, and even though she knew she was standing, her legs were still invisible to her.

"I still can't see them. What should we do?"

Dave had no answer, so he smiled to make Meg believe all was okay while he tried to figure out what was going on.

"Maybe we're in some kind of alternate virtual universe, and our vision signals are mixed up. I'm not sure everything we're experiencing is constructive for the game's goals. I don't know how making parts invisible is helpful in any way. Making us *totally* invisible to others should be helpful, but parts?"

Dave was still trying to convince himself this was a game. His doubts increased each minute. In the last game, there had been no separations from the kids, no injuries, and no vision problems. They figured things out by using logic and reasoning to solve their predicaments. They always received high marks for their problem-solving skills when their actions were evaluated at their game exit conferences.

* * *

Terrence, Tony, and Ralph sat in quiet observation back at AstroSPAN. Terrence spoke first.

"I'm glad to see Meg can actually stand. That EnCapturator gimmick had me worried at first. I wasn't sure if wiping out her vision of her legs only wiped out her vision or actually destroyed her legs. "Why can Dave still see her legs? What good is an invisibility technique if it affects only the person we zap? I know I didn't activate the EnCapturator, so which one of you guys did?"

Tony looked like he was about to answer, but stopped. Ralph looked totally blank, a look he had perfected over the years. Terrence waited a second, and then he asked again, "Okay, guys, what gives?"

Ralph answered first. "Uh, I was about to ask you the same thing. I didn't touch anything. I figured it was one of you guys." He turned to look at Tony.

Tony decided to go with the truth. "I was told to trip that switch without you guys knowing. But guess what? I decided not to do it. We've never tried it before, and I was afraid it would permanently destroy its target—Meg's legs. I couldn't bring myself to do it. Just couldn't. I failed."

Ralph and Terrence, in unison, sputtered, "Then who did?"

15

Beyond the Known Truth

The AstroSPAN control room sat in the middle of the TriTopTechRun Game Campus, hidden from access to anyone not part of the inner circle of the game hierarchy. Complex labyrinths were designed when the games began, and further architectural additions made access to any outsiders impossible. The control room had no windows. It used artificial light sources to mimic daylight, with multiple access codes and eye-recognition screenings throughout the complex, so any intrusions would be prevented.

Terrence, Tony, and Ralph were in place this Thursday, in front of their bank of video screens for their daily monitoring exercises. The room had become more crowded over the past three years as the tech hardware and software improved and more inventions were put into operation. Whenever anyone asked Terrence what he did for a living, he said he dusted the insides of gigantic computers so our planet stays in its orbit. He loved the way people always laughed at this response, not knowing how close it was to the truth. Hiding in plain sight was a tactic he put to good use.

The three Guides had been on the job for two hours when the outer door to the control room flew open. Terrence was the first Guide to respond. He swiveled in his chair, ready to stand and face whomever or whatever had entered. He reached for his cell phone to call Command-Six to warn them his office had been breached, but his hand never reached his phone. He tried to scream for help, but no sound came out. He was frozen in place. A mysterious power prevented any movement. He knew he needed to react, but his thoughts were scrambled. The only things he could move were his eyes. They had opened wide and stuck that way. He turned them toward Tony and Ralph's chairs.

Tony had jumped up at the sound of the door opening, but he made it only halfway to a standing position when his body felt a force immobilize him. Ralph was a half second behind Tony and Terrence in his reaction. The same invisible force held him in his chair. He could not stand or react further.

An overpowering need to move enveloped

Tony, but like the others, he remained frozen. His head cleared slightly after the initial impact.

Two men invaded the room. They were dressed alike: bright-red, super-tight clothing, much like Spider-Man costumes, minus the webs, and silver masks covering only their eyes. A small insignia was on their left shoulders in the shape of a with-ered tree with two dark-blue letters, which were not clear at this distance. Each invader held a shiny pen-like object. Terrence assumed the pens were the source of the disabling power that had seized his body.

Think. Think. This can't be happening. There is no way they have broken through our three layers of secu-rity inside our building and four layers of mine fields, surrounded by moats, outside. This must be a revolt by personnel working with us. We are fail-safe. I know we are fail-safe.

"How adorable you look. Frozen like frosty popsicles. One more squeeze on this pen and you'll melt down into your shoes, like strawberry ice cream on a summer day!" He had a wicked, turned-down sneer just below his bushy mustache. He kept a steady hold on his pen.

"And you all thought you were so smart and nothing could get in here. Wrong!"

Let me think. Has to be a way out of this. Terrence saw Ralph and Tony's eyes were fixed, staring straight ahead. They remained frozen. Terrence was careful not to let the intruders see his eyes shift ever so slightly; he had closed the lids to a narrow slit. Desperate for a solution to this intrusion, Terrence thought, *Let's find out if those boring mind-lessons can help solve this.*

That entire training cycle had bored Terrence. He'd paid close attention to the instruction, but he thought it was some silly hocus-pocus their trainers had used to get them to build confidence in themselves. Terrence always placed his confidence in what he could directly see or touch. He was a highly trained and rational warrior, skilled in real weaponry and logical problem solving.

Terrence believed in talent and dedication, not magic. He was a good multitasker and could always think about something else and still pay attention to the lessons.

He had to act. He was glad he didn't have to work to hold himself still; the force, whatever it was, held him steady in its grasp. Terrence burrowed his eyes directly into the barrel of the pen closest to him. He felt like he was actually inside the pen. He tried hard to remember the magic words they'd learned. *How did it go? Aha! That's it!*

Inside, Outside
Upside, Downside
Power Send, Power Bend
Skirmish End, Change to Friend!

He chanted it twice in his head, then blinked his eyes once, hoping no one perceived the blink. No sooner did he speak the last word in his brain than the pen exploded with a puff of purple smoke and jumped from the hand of the intruder to land softly in Terrence's palm. Terrence felt his body returning to normal. Ralph and Tony's bodies resumed their previous positions as well. No one seemed any worse for wear.

The two intruders patted each other on their backs and advanced toward Terrence, enormous smiles on their faces, thanking him for releasing them from their captivity, talking to Terrence like he was an old friend. They all high-fived each other. Foes a few minutes ago became BFFs. Terrence asked who sent them. They talked over each other in a rush to tell how they had been detained by the ShrinkWithers' main officers and sent to carry out complex captures of highly placed AstroSPAN commanders, in order to gain information about their experiments and inventions.

Any doubts about the value of his training disappeared. This turn of events was bizarre, but Terrence had learned a valuable new lesson. He no longer felt that only things he could see, touch, and taste were real. Perhaps things unseen were part of another reality. A helpful one.

Terrence told himself his new mantra would be, *"We don't know everything about everything."* While he had managed to turn this disaster around, he knew his larger question—Who's trying to sabotage the games?—had now been answered. The ShrinkWithers had upped their game, and the battle for Earth's resources and welfare had begun.

16

Lies, All Lies

Jenny suddenly felt hot and shaky. She was super-happy to have Branch back in her sight, clinging to the outside of the bubble, but her anxiety increased. She couldn't imagine how Branch was going to release them from the bubble. Or how they would make it back to the ground without another capture. Her mind raced. She was losing faith in their eventual success. She needed to relax. Seven was her lucky number, so she tried to settle her nerves by counting slowly to seven before she spoke again.

Branch watched Jenny count, her lips mouthing each number, remembering she always counted when she was uneasy. She had even helped him sometimes at night when he had an awful dream, telling him to count until he felt better. He saw she might be losing her courage. He waited quietly, with a fake grin on his face to show her his confidence.

As she said "seven," Jenny snapped back to reality, returned Branch's smile with one of her own, and burst out with, "That's it! That's it, Branch!"

"What, Jen?"

"I've got it! Check your pockets. Hang on tight to the bubble. Don't let go! Remember that small plastic sandwich baggie Mom gave you right before school started? You know, the one she said would be your lucky charm for the school year? She said to keep the bag with you, day and night—through thick and thin. And we are definitely in a thin part right now. Do you still have it?"

Each September, their mom had given Branch a tiny plastic bag to keep with him every day. This year's baggie held a safety pin, a sesame seed, and a paper octopus tattoo. Branch had assumed there was nothing magic about it, thinking it was just one of his mom's fun psychology tricks to help him *think positive* and build confidence in his ability to handle any problems that might arise. Now, he wondered.

"And you think this is the sort of problem Mom meant?"

"Precisely!" said Jen.

"Okay, Jen, what's your strategy? Don't expect me to believe there's a connection between a safety pin, a sesame seed, an octopus sticker tattoo, and our problems right now."

"Don't you see, Branch? I think Mom knew exactly what she was doing. Those three things might be tickets to saving us. I'm going to focus on the safety pin and the sesame seed. You concentrate on the octopus tattoo. Try to imagine how it can help us.

"First, we need a way out of this bubble. Second, we need to land somewhere safe, either on the ground or a body of water near the shore. Third, remember the ShrinkWithers probably will be watching us. We'll need invisible protective coverings, plus a worthy vessel for travel once we touch down."

"You're not asking for much, are you? Just the moon and the stars with whipped cream and a chocolate cherry on top. Fine. No problem. I'll whip that right up in my cosmic kitchen. Should only take a sec. Now, where did I hide my magic potion-motion blender?"

"I know it's a lot to expect, Branch. But look what we've accomplished this time, none of which we knew beforehand. We used our wits and made progress. We managed to survive. No matter what came our way."

Jenny and Branch stopped talking in order to think. A combination of their own logical abilities, along with a few touches of magic, had always helped them in the games since the beginning. They knew magic aided them sometimes, but neither one could pinpoint when it would kick in. Sometimes they'd summon it by thinking, or they'd try a chant. It didn't always work. Their wits were their most reliable protection.

Where normal life stopped and fantasy magic began was never an exact line for either of them. Things just seemed to happen. Some of their responses had worked so far, but it was frustrating not always having control over what, where, and especially when.

Were they just lucky? Or were they truly endowed with super powers?

Time was important. Jenny and Branch fell silent, focusing on their task items. *Safety pin. Sesame seed. Octopus tattoo. Concentrate.* What was Mom trying to tell them?

Jenny waved her hands at Branch in excitement. Deep in thought, Branch took a few seconds to realize she was motioning to him.

"Stop it, Jenny! I need to focus."

"I've got it, Branch! I've got it!"

"What?!" Branch was irritated to be interrupted. He was also upset that he had no answers yet and Jenny did. He had begun to feel proud of his accomplishments in this game and happy that he could compete along with Jenny and gain her admiration. Branch wanted to be first to figure a way to use the tattoo.

"It's so easy, I'm almost embarrassed to say it. The safety pin. We need to float safely back to Earth. What could be easier than poking a tiny hole in our bubble? Up at the top, below your right hand. Give it a quick poke. It'll allow air at the top of the bubble to escape and give us power from the air escaping our bubble as we float slowly earthward. Then, once you've poked that hole, you can teleport yourself inside the bubble so we go down together. You're making me so nervous, clinging precariously to the outside."

"How do we know we'll descend slowly and land where we need to? Whenever I've popped a balloon, it's gone out of control, twisted madly, and landed in a limp heap faster than you could say pop!"

Branch pictured them lying in a sad, mangled crumple on the ground, like day-after birthday party balloons.

"We don't, but this bubble is obviously made of a powerful material, much stronger than a balloon. And with all the pressure balance of the liquid and air inside, versus the outside air pressure, it should take time to descend—hopefully enough time to plop us down with a marshmallow-soft landing.

"What do you think, Branch?" Jenny counted on Branch's okay to make her feel confident the plan would succeed.

"I'm all for marshmallow-soft. We'll need transport when we land. Plus, our transport must be both water-worthy and land-legit, for both probabilities. You're ahead of me, Jen. I haven't got the tattoo part solved yet."

This bothered Jen, but she decided to waste no more time worrying and moved on to the sesame seed part of the puzzle, leaving Branch to solve the tattoo transport problem.

Sesame seeds, safety pins, and tattoos. Who would'a thought?

17

Listen to Dad

Dave decided it was time to act. He was done with overthinking. Done with worrying about the planners and doers of the game. As exciting as their participation had been last year, the thrill was gone now. There were too many unanswered questions and near misses. Doom and gloom were the patterns of his family's lives in this game. Dave wondered if the Guides could hear him if he spoke aloud. He knew they watched everything on their screens, but he wasn't sure if they could hear everything. He didn't want the enemy ShrinkWithers to hear, but he decided to risk a shout to the Guides for help.

"We're in over our heads here! Intervention please! I can't watch my family getting hurt!"

Ominous signs, threats of failure, and injury peered at them around each corner. No earlier training had prepared them for the pop-up emergencies happening in this game. Branch and Jenny had always been nearby in previous adventures. This time it seemed like they all were deliberately being kept apart. The stress of not knowing if the kids were safe was something Dave never wanted to experience again. *That's too much to ask. Let another family be the guinea pigs next time.*

For the past fifteen years, Dave had been committed to addressing climate change in his professional life. Because of his advanced studies in oceanography, along with Earth and atmospheric sciences, he was sought after for consulting with governments and companies developing policy and technology. His alarm at the rapid rate of deterioration of our planet's air, water, and land quality led him to join a secret think tank operation several years back, to prevent a disaster of mega proportions. One step had led to another, and collaboration with clever people of all ages created these practice survival competitions to explore new ways to combat the loss of our planet's resources and lives. The games were created to assess technological and psychological advancements. Dave had signed on to the early investigations by himself, in hopes of making the world safer for his family and all families. When the TriTopTechRun games began, he included his family in the effort, hoping to provide good strategies for them.

But now Dave decided to just say no to any future involvement with AstroSPAN, no matter how much they pleaded. Enough. Not worth it. *Saving my family must come first from now on. Humanity can fend for itself.* What had seemed a good idea now frightened him and hurt his family.

"Meg, listen up. Forget the leg stuff. We're moving on. If we use our last item in the knapsack, maybe we can code in Jenny and Branch's IDs and pick up their communication wavelengths."

Meg gasped. She knew what he was about to do. He reached for the backpack and slipped his right hand into the secret pocket sewn into the cavity, near the bottom of the outside flap. He almost managed to grab the tiny silver thing that resembled a harmonica.

Meg gathered all her strength and dived at Dave's legs, knocking him off his feet, landing them both in the dirt. She had one elbow on his chest to hold him down. Guess what? That was working really well. He couldn't move a muscle, couldn't get any air in or out, and had to drop the object because he needed both hands to fend off Meg's assault.

Meg's sudden violence took Dave by surprise. He was slow to respond with enough strength to defend himself against Meg's angry takedown. She raised her other arm high in the air. Just as her karate chop to his neck was about to knock him unconscious, he went limp, and in one quick movement, dropped out of her hold and snapped upright to his knees.

Something was very wrong. They'd never been at odds before. What was wrong with Meg? They both scrambled to their feet.

"Stop, Dave! They trained us never to use the I-Sponder—only as a last resort, if we or others were severely injured. Are you forgetting they warned us it hasn't been through all its control tests? They said they weren't able to predict all possible effects. They included it in our pack only for an absolute emergency!"

"Stop, Meg. I know. I considered that before reaching for it. It's been too long since this part of the game has started. We don't know if Branch and Jen are safe. This is the longest we've been apart since they recruited us the first time. I don't see any way out, except to activate the I-Sponder, whether or not it's safe. We're stuck here. The kids may be in grave danger. We have no more answers. Desperate circumstances require desperate means."

"Dave, I can't bring myself to try it. What if it sets off something that destroys us? Or destroys Jenny and Branch? Or wipes out this entire area? What then? Our kids will have no help at all. No one to act for them. No one to bring them back home safely. They're smart, but they're not ready to raise themselves!"

"I repeat, Meg, we have no choice. No answers. Nothing else to try."

Meg could not slow her breathing. The

adrenaline rushing through her body from the panic of seeing no way to help her kids was slow to vanish. It had taken all her energy to combat the man she loved. Her fears for Jenny and Branch gave her super-strength for a short moment. Her mindset didn't match her husband's yet.

"Dave, give me a minute."

Dave busied himself pretending to organize the contents of the backpack, carefully avoiding the secret compartment. Meg's eyes followed his movements, making sure he was not touching that area. Dave couldn't afford another one of Meg's superwoman stunts. She might knock him out the next time. The Guides hadn't answered his plea.

Dave thought about their training. He saw no options except to take the I-Sponder out fast, figure a way to activate it, and hope. He put on his trust-me-I've-got-everything-under-control face and whispered.

"Okay, Meg. It's time. I'll remove the I-Sponder from the backpack. We'll study it, talk about it, and hope it'll help us. We've got to do something *now*. There's no more time." He looked at the ground as he waited for Meg to agree.

Meg had no better idea to try because she didn't see any solutions. Her nerves were shot. Brain freeze had set in. Not having any other answers, she gave in to Dave.

"Okay, Dave. It's your call. Let's try to figure it out." Meg looked sincere and focused, but she was shaking with doubt.

18

By a Thread

*W*e *don't know everything about everything.*

Terrence reviewed his new mantra and yesterday's threatening events as he slid into his chair the next morning. He had contacted the security forces and reported yesterday's strange break-in. Terrence was pleased to see the new door replacement and was certain extra security was in place. He knew they had made it through a close call. What didn't fit? Who was behind the intruders? He and his fellow staff were the top Guides for the games. They were the most competent and dedicated AstroSPAN engineers. Their quarters had never been breached. They were safe for now, but even with the intruders magically rescued and turned into friends, plus his newfound faith in the unseen, he was still uneasy.

Any good brainstorm ideas had evaded him throughout the night, and so had sleep. He'd tossed and turned, waking up exhausted. He drove too fast to work, intent on talking with Ralph and Tony throughout the day, hoping to piece together some answers.

"Whoa, didn't you go home last night?" Ralph asked Terrence.

"Whaddya mean?" Terrence shot Ralph a startled look.

"Look at yourself. You wore those same clothes yesterday—your Cubs shirt and khakis."

Terrence looked down at his clothes and grinned when he saw they were yesterday's clothes. He vaguely remembered being so worn out after the break-in yesterday that when he got home, he fell into bed still dressed. He remembered sleeping restlessly, waking and checking the clock through the night, eventually passing out around five this morning. When the alarm rang at six thirty, there was no time to shower and change clothes. He thought it best to show up on time to work out a plan.

"Yeah, I do look like a nightmare. Why aren't there any images on our screens?"

Terrence sat back in his chair, tilting it to where it looked impossible to stay upright. Just like his life—on the edge. They listed their guesses on who, what, and why yesterday's intrusion happened.

Tony started. "What's the first thing you noticed when those guys burst in?"

"Who had time to notice anything? I was frozen in my tracks. I don't remember a thing until we woke up and those fools were smiling and shaking our hands and patting our backs. I thought they were new recruits. I had no clue at first. How about you, Ralph?"

While Terrence and Tony had been talking, Ralph had been wracking his brain, trying to wake up his cloudy memory of the previous day, searching for anything that would make sense. He wasn't used to being out of ideas. When Ralph finally responded, he spat out his words in quick succession.

"I got nothin'. Absolutely nothin', guys. Only a vague memory of lookin' at those two vicious guys staring at us, a tiny pen thing exploding, and everything going dark. I have no memory from that point on until the smiles and friendly comments. What did they do? Hire new techs? Are they our replacements? Have they fired us? Why isn't there anything on our screens this morning?"

Right in the middle of Ralph's questions, Tony got up from his chair, straightened papers on his desk, and walked slowly toward the door. Terrence glanced up at him and looked back at Ralph, waiting for him to continue. Ralph jumped up from his chair and dived toward Tony, his entire body extended flat-out in a tackle. His arms reached out to take Tony down. They fell in a heap on the floor, Ralph smashed on top of Tony.

"Holy cow, guys! What's going on?" Terrence was not prepared to handle any crazy stuff today. He was worn out from the invasion yesterday. Now this.

"Lock the door, Terrence!" Ralph shouted, holding Tony tightly, preventing his escape.

Terrence raced toward the door and slid the electronic safety bar over the lock mechanism. He spun around to see Tony twist out of Ralph's arms and flip to a standing position, holding a small laser weapon aimed right at Terrence's chest.

"Whoa, Tony, drop that thing. You're out of your mind right now. Think, man, think!"

Terrence was sure Tony was having a reaction to yesterday's freezing episode. Maybe there'd been a chemical infused into their bodies when the silver pen exploded, something that took effect hours later.

"Cut it, guys! You don't get it, do you? I'm taking over this operation. I have people on the outside ready to blast in here. AstroSPAN has been outlawed by the ShrinkWithers. You're under our control now. Yesterday's episode froze you for two hours, long enough for the new team to enter, reprogram all the safety options, change the passwords, and prepare for Operation TakeDown. Earth, its minerals, its water sources, its plant and animal life—ours, all ours from now on!"

"You've gotta be kidding! What's wrong with

you? We three have worked together for eleven years. We three are the commanders who guide these trials to success, with nobody injured. What's your reason for mutiny, Tony?" Ralph hoped to stall long enough until he could figure how to get the laser out of Tony's hand.

"Shut up! I don't have to answer any of your questions. Time to go!"

Tony pressed the trigger on the laser. The room lit up like a Fourth of July fireworks display. Then everything went dark. Terrence and Ralph collapsed.

Tony smiled, thrilled to see Ralph and Terrence unconscious on the floor. He felt a surge of supreme power, free from those years of pretending—playing two roles, always taking orders. He was almost successful yesterday, but that didn't go according to plan because the ShrinkWither intruder had accidently hit him with the immobilizing pen. He'd thought they were smarter than that.

19

Safety Pin, Tattoo, Sesame Seed—Yes!

Branch knew they could think better if they were on the ground. The water sloshing inside the sphere and the movement of the sphere through the atmosphere made his stomach queasy. Without saying a word to Jenny, he put her plan into action. He hung on tight and reached down toward the plastic casing.

He shouted, "We're going down NOW!"

Branch put all his strength into his right shoulder, lifted his arm high, and poked the safety pin through the top of the sphere.

The sphere reacted swiftly and started a slow drift to earth, gently swinging left, then right, making wide arcs in a rhythmic pattern, using the escaping air for power. Their descent was smooth and steady.

Jenny, engrossed in trying to solve the sesame seed part of the puzzle, hadn't sensed they were going down. When the tips of the tallest pines came into view, she realized they were getting close to earth. Happy that it appeared they were slowly drifting toward an area of thick pines, she began to feel safe. She clapped her hands and said, "F-a-n-t-a-s . . ." to Branch when their balloon took a sudden arc upward.

"Branch! What's happening? Why are we going up again?"

Branch had no answer for Jen. He'd enjoyed the relaxed calm for those few seconds of drifting, when it seemed like they'd achieve their marshmallow-soft landing. He looked at Jen with a blank expression.

Their mouths dropped open when they realized they'd changed course. Instead of continuing their course to earth, they were heading out to sea, approximately three-hundred feet above the surface of the Atlantic, moving along at a fast clip, a nautical mile out from shore. The wind picked up. Branch figured their dwindling balloon had gone from traveling slowly to almost two hundred feet per second.

"Yikes!" Branch shouted. "We were doing so well, all set to land on those treetops."

"I know. We'll be in England in a few hours

at this rate. Much as I'd love to visit Buckingham Palace, we're way off course." Jenny tried to hide her panic. *Only one thing to do.*

Jenny snatched the safety pin from her brother and held it up toward the original hole he'd made in the sphere. She jabbed it into the surface, twisting it around and around until the hole tore open much wider. Their forward motion slowed, but the seawater was coming up faster. She grabbed Branch's hand through the larger opening, pulling him safely next to her inside the sphere. Jenny figured they'd land in the sea in about seventy-five seconds.

Desperate to save their lives, but out of ideas, Jenny placed the tattoo on the top of her wrist, concentrating on its adorable little octopus picture. Ten seconds went by. Jenny focused harder. She began to whisper a countdown of the number of seconds she estimated it would take to get to their landing, which looked like it was going to be rough.

"38 – 37 – 36 – 35 – 34 – 33 – 32 – 31 . . ." As she said thirty-one, the tattoo became hot and expanded. Jenny grabbed Branch's hand tighter. "Hang on, Branch! Hang on tight!"

She closed her eyes and held tight to Branch's hand, hoping he would not slip away. So much water in their sphere. Water rushing at them from the ocean. Water gushing up their noses. They were pressed hard against the inside of the sphere. She closed her eyes to protect them and hoped Branch did, too.

What's that sound?

Laughter. A long laugh that didn't stop for air.

Branch was laughing hard. *What a fabulous sound!* Followed by the sound of the remaining water in the sphere being pulled out with a huge swoosh, Jenny and Branch along with it, into the ocean.

Jenny felt her whole body rise and something slimy underneath her feet. Jenny and Branch—hands scrunched together like a knot that would never come undone—found themselves sprawled on top of a giant red octopus, its arms pumping them safely toward the shore like a steamship. Full speed ahead! Going from the peace and quiet of the sphere to this lively transportation was a roller-coaster ride never imagined.

20

I Spy, You Spy,
We All Spy

Meg and Dave knew it would be dark soon. They welcomed it so they could take advantage of better cover. They aimed for the general direction they guessed Branch had gone, but they were not sure it was correct. Dave reached into the bottom of the backpack, looking for a break in the stitching that would let his fingers pull open the secret flap. It was hard for Meg not to push him aside and do it herself. Her sense of urgency usually trumped his sense of patience, but this time she waited. Dave found an opening, wiggled his thumbnail, and pulled out several more stitches, permitting him access to the tiny silver I-Sponder.

It was a small cylinder, three inches long, with tiny buttons lining two opposite sides and one slightly larger press-key at the bottom. It felt heavy for its size and cool to the touch. He hoped it could help them.

"Give it here, Dave. Those buttons are tiny and too close together for your large fingers to click on."

"Sure, Meg. Be careful not to press anything until we figure out what's what."

Meg was irritated at Dave's warning, but let it pass.

This would be a challenge. If they made excellent choices, they could improve their situation and reach the kids. If not . . .

She and Dave dropped to the ground, so if the I-Sponder fell, it didn't have far to go. Meg gently turned it over and over in her hand, careful not to press any buttons. She noticed there were no letters or numbers on its surface.

Dave watched closely as the I-Sponder rolled over in Meg's hand. He was alert to any perceived pattern in the placement of the buttons on its sides. Something seemed familiar.

"Meg, slow down. Turn it over and look at the side that just rolled under. What does that remind you of?"

Meg turned the cylinder until they saw the row that had tucked under. There were three dot-buttons close together at one end, followed by a break, then two dot-buttons and one dash, another break, and finally, a dash and three dot-buttons at the other end.

••• ••— —•••

Meg sat still, peering at the cylinder. She sighed. Then she stared. She wrinkled her forehead, squinting her eyes, hoping to cause the button puzzle to reveal its secret. Nope. Nothing.

"I've got nothing, Dave. It's an interesting pattern, but has no meaning for me." Meg looked at Dave and responded to his grin. "Obviously, you see something. Let me in on it."

"Meg, remember our training days? It's Morse code, a communication system first used in 1844. Alphabet letters were represented by a series of dots and dashes that traveled over a wire to a receiver on the other end. It took a while to decode, but the system worked in many wars, starting with our Civil War, where it helped Abraham Lincoln."

"Good grief, Dave. We're wasting lots of time with you turning on your professor voice. Get to the point."

Dave's laugh helped settle their nerves for a moment. "We're in high-tech days now, and this seems dated, so maybe we shouldn't rely on it. But here we are, out of touch with our usual electronic devices, dependent only on our own ingenuity. Back to basics might be our only choice if we face a lack of electronics in some situations in the future."

Checking the cylinder once more, the dots and dashes suddenly made sense. The first three dots represented an S, the two dots with the dash made a U, and the last bunch—one dash and three dots—were a B. There it was! S-U-B.

Meg and Dave said the word "SUB" at the same instant.

Meg spoke first. "Fine and dandy. Now what? There are buttons to push and buttons spelling out the word SUB. We're stranded with two worn-out brains, and our kids are who knows where."

Thinking this additional information important in the next part of the game, Dave had to make things happen—now. He jumped to his feet and started doing jumping jacks.

Meg was startled. This husband of hers, the father of their two fabulous kids, was doing vigorous jumping jacks out here in the forest while they were trying not to call attention to themselves.

"Dave, stop it. This is crazy! Have you gone off the deep end? What's happening to you?"

Dave jumped faster, ignoring Meg's plea to stop.

"Dave. Stop it!"

Meg held on tightly to the I-Sponder, fearing Dave would grab it and hit the random buttons, smashing them, and their chance to help their kids, to smithereens.

Dave's eyes glazed. He made one final leap, going high in the air, coming down to a crouch, exhaling heavily, pumping oxygen in and out of his lungs quickly. Then he jumped up and began whirling.

Meg moved farther out of the way, protecting

the cylinder by increasing her distance from this madman called Dave.

She needed to prepare herself for what might happen next. She feared Dave was exhibiting signs of breakdown. He might harm her or himself. Feeling alone and terrified, her arms quivered and her legs wobbled. Her eyes narrowed. She tried to plan an escape that would save her in an emergency, but not harm Dave. She feared she might have to betray Dave to save herself—that was the hardest thought of all.

Meg slipped the I-Sponder into her shirt pocket, being sure to button the pocket flap over it. She'd dash in the only direction workable, back the way they came, since she didn't know what lay ahead. She could outrun Dave on a normal day, but his present state of distress had shot loads of adrenaline into his body. She didn't know if that would help him or make him fade more quickly. This was unfamiliar territory for her and Dave, a territory she had no wish to navigate alone.

One of them had to get to the kids, even if it meant leaving the other behind. She consoled herself, knowing Dave would make the same decision if she were behaving this way and endangering them.

21

Out of Answers

Terrence and Ralph woke slowly, discovering they were lying on the floor of the observation room of AstroSPAN, where they'd landed when the laser hit them, knocking them unconscious. Terrence struggled to get upright, and when he finally managed it, he tilted to one side, his legs weak. Ralph, still groggy, wasn't certain where they were, but he was glad to be conscious and to see Terrence awake beside him.

"Where's Tony?" Ralph murmured.

Terrence didn't respond promptly. He was trying to remember why they were on the floor and what had taken place. Then it all came back to him.

"Tony did it! Tony zapped us with that laser. I

remember nothing after that." Terrence's remarks were coming in brief spurts as he came to.

"Exactly! That's the last thing I recall before we were knocked out. He sure fooled us all these years. I can't believe he turned traitor. I was so shocked he was aiming at us. By the time I realized what was happening, it was too late."

Ralph thought of the years the three of them had worked as a team, dedicated to greater knowledge and establishing safe operating methods, devoted to their cause. He couldn't think of their trusted coworker as an enemy, regardless of what Tony had done to them.

"Does this qualify, Terrence?"

"What do you mean?"

"Does this qualify as an 'extenuating circumstance,' where we have no other option than to use Plan Sesame Seed?"

Ralph waited until Terrence's face lost its shocked look. Terrence couldn't believe what his ears had just heard. Plan Sesame Seed. No one believed this apocalyptic last-chance-to-save-the-universe option was ever to be used in these game trials. Everyone thought of it as a training joke, something the designers devised to provide them with an end-of-life-as-we-know-it fantasy. They figured if trainees saw these adventures as a game, they could handle their fears better.

Sometimes when they were bored or had free time, trainees played a game of coming up with wild scenarios. They'd suggest outlandishly complex solutions and call them a variety of names, each one trying to surpass the next person in absurdity: Plan Weevil-Upheaval, Plan Clammy-Whammy, Plan Creepy-Crawler-Staller, Plan Sinister-StarWar-Monger, Plan Robot-Regurgitate, Plan Cringer-Avenger.

But to think they should choose to carry out Plan Sesame Seed at this moment? No! This couldn't be happening.

How could this be happening?

Ralph asked, "Do you think we need to stop the game now? The players are working outside their comfort zones, way outside their training roles. They're showing behaviors we've never seen. Something's not right. We can't control the outcomes. There's been a takeover. We don't even know if our AstroSpan Masters are still in place. We know nothing outside of this room. Are we in game land or real land? What's wrong with Dave? Why has Meg dashed off alone? I fear we're close to losing some of our finest designer-participants—either by some sinister disaster in this year's session, or by Dave and his family withdrawing their participation from now on."

Ignoring Ralph's questions, Terrence silently practiced his plea to the Masters, so that he'd get a sensible answer and all would be well. He concentrated on his mantra to calm himself down, running it over and over in his head.

We don't know everything about everything.

It didn't work to calm him. He remained

agitated. He was out of answers and out of his usual confidence in a safe conclusion. Something was not as it should be. Why and what?

22

Two If By Sea, and Cephalopod Makes Three

"**P**repare for landing!" shouted Branch in his finest ship-captain voice.

When the octopus tattoo had expanded into a *real octopus,* Branch and Jenny found themselves sitting on top of it as they all landed in the ocean. They still gripped hands, struggling not to slip off the slimy octopus as they hurtled across the water. Branch shouted to Jenny that octopus appendages are called arms, not tentacles, and a giant Pacific octopus can have 2,240 suction cups total. He looked so smug when he said it. Jenny was happy to be held in them, regardless of what they were called and how many there were.

Branch could make out large letters painted or tattooed on the octopus. They were below him and upside down to his position, but he could identify them, except for the two letters on the other side of Jenny.

"Jenny, when I say the names of the letters I see, carefully look below and over to your left and tell me what you see. Hold tight! Don't change your position. I see O-L-I-V. What's on your side, Jen?"

Jenny blinked several times to remove the water from her eyes.

"I see I-A," Jenny said. "O-L-I-V-I-A. I bet that's her name. Olivia the Octopus."

The minute Jenny said "Olivia" aloud, the octopus raised arms four and eight, clasping them together over her body like a knock-out boxer.

Branch cheered. "Wow! She knows her name. And she's happy we figured it out."

Branch and Jenny turned their attention back to their surroundings. Hanging on was their major issue now since the sea had become choppy and bigger waves were battering them as they made their way to shore. If it weren't for Olivia's sticky skin, they'd lose their grips.

Olivia was extremely powerful, but she swam slower now, due to the surge of the waves.

They were still clipping along far too fast for comfort, but the sooner they reached land, the better. Branch estimated they'd reach the shore in less than five minutes. He wanted Jenny to be forewarned of what might be a dreadful end to their wild octopus ride. He dropped Jenny's hand so he could turn completely around to survey the octopus, the water, the shoreline, and the sky, to try to avoid disaster.

He screamed his warning. "Prepare for landing!"

"Another of your kid jokes, Branch? How should I prepare? Do I prefer to go in head-first? Feet-first, maybe? Elbow-first? I've never tried that one. I'm fresh out of brilliant ideas. Just *sitting* on this cephalopod has me terrified, much less racing this fast. Look out! Isn't that shoreline made of solid rock? Right at the edge where it looks like we'll land."

Branch noticed the rocks while Jenny listed body-part landing options with her usual sarcasm. He twisted away from watching the shoreline to scan the octopus, head to arm—all eight of them. *Arm five. That's it!* He scrambled over to arm five, grabbing Jenny's hand once more, pulled them both into the underside of the thickest part of the arm's biggest suction cups, and shouted to Jenny, "Hide in here! Don't let go!"

He slid into the suction cups under another large arm.

Jenny clung tight. She intended to heed Branch's warning not to let go, but the octopus ejected slimy purple ink over Jenny and Branch as they burrowed into its suction cups. The slippery ink slathered over both of them, making it tough to hold on to anything, especially their courage.

If it weren't for the powerful suction of the cups holding them inside, they would have slid into the ocean. The ink smelled like a combination of seaweed, rotten fish, and kitchen garbage. In spite of that nasty odor, it relieved them to be caught up in Olivia's magical arms. They snuggled inside, feeling like Mom and Dad were holding them.

Olivia's arms scooped Branch and Jenny back and forth as she aimed toward shore, jerking her arms for propulsion. The ink prevented them from seeing if they were going to smash against the giant rocks or land gently on soft sand.

Exactly at the moment in which Jenny and Branch ran out of hope for a secure landing due to their speed, Olivia reversed her body position in the water, stretched out each arm toward the shore, and came to a jarring stop. Her landing was still a jolt, but her arms absorbed the impact as they hit a sandy stretch between two of the largest rock piles. Branch and Jenny felt nothing stronger than the force of one of their jumps off the fourth step in their hallway at home whenever they were running late for the school bus.

Jenny feared moving at first. She knew it was awesome they had landed gently, but what an impossible task it would be to get that goopy ink off. Maybe they should follow the octopus back to the ocean to see if the force of the waves could wash the ink away. Olivia turned back toward them when she reached the edge of the beach. She lifted arm six high in the air, and magic! All the slime pulled away from their skin and clothing and absorbed back into Olivia.

Jenny sighed and added this miracle to the imaginary list she kept in her head—the list entitled "Things That Won't Ever Happen, But Sometimes Do, When The Stars Are Just Right, and I Am Really Desperate."

Jenny plopped down on the beach to think. "Branch, nothing's making sense. I'm struggling to tie it together, to figure out what the purpose of this challenge is. We aren't accomplishing anything that seems worthwhile. We go from danger to danger and then escape, but so what? How's this helping our world improve?"

"It's bothering me, too. Is someone toying with us, keeping us away from the actual game quest? Is it a takeover? The end of life as we know it? Are we combatting the game planners or the ShrinkWithers in these setbacks? I have no clue."

"Okay, Branch, cut it out. We can't both be dreary. I'd hoped you'd make better sense of this than I can. Let's get off the beach. We're targets out here in the open. Let's take shelter in that boathouse, to think and share our ideas."

After their recent adventures up in the air and down in the ocean, Jenny realized Branch was indispensable to their success and survival. She knew this was the perfect moment to let him know she appreciated him and his help.

"Branch, I used to see you as someone I had to take care of. Now I see you as my equal. You're still annoying, of course, but I certainly value your judgment and actions on this trip. We make a great team. I couldn't have survived without you. I'll probably regret this later, but right now . . . YOU DA' MAN, LITTLE BRO!"

Jenny blushed, but while she felt strange admitting it to Branch, she knew it was the proper time to tell him. He'd earned her praise.

About time! Branch almost blurted out his first thought but caught himself and just looked down at the ground, not knowing how to respond. He wasn't sure he was okay with Jen treating him with such respect. He had played second trumpet in her band for so many years that he was more comfortable with her put-downs than her build-ups.

Team. That's the word she used. He knew he was far from her equal, but now he realized he had navigated a huge barrier between them, no longer limited by who was born first, who was a girl or a boy, or who was smarter.

They could collaborate. They'd withstand their challenges if they stuck together. He should let her know he was grateful for her praise, but his ego overtook him.

He answered with his little brother boastful shout, "Yes! I always knew I was the best!"

23

If Only I Could

Meg watched as Dave spun frantically around. Because he faced away from her during part of each spin, Meg struggled to check his eyes. When she caught a glimpse, she saw no recognition in them.

Dave's jumping jacks picked up speed, his arms thrashing wildly. Meg had no clue how he could whirl around so fast while doing jumping jacks. There was a robotic rhythm to his movements.

His legs snapped awkwardly to what sounded like the bizarre music of an evil wizard determined to whirl Dave into the ground. His eyes were wide open, but they never focused on hers—not once.

He was spinning so fast it was impossible to time her escape dash to the precise moment he faced away. Meg took in a huge gulp of air and made a gigantic leap back up the trail, the way they had come.

This vault maneuver would have worked on an ordinary day. Today, it failed miserably.

She leaped toward the trail but felt Dave's hand tighten on hers just as a wind of hurricane proportions swept them both off their feet, blinding them with its fury. She gasped, "Oh, no!" as water and dust clogged her mouth with soggy grit, drowning out further sound.

Right before she passed out, Meg remembered there was something besides Dave's hand that she should hang on to. She thought, *If only I could remem . . .*

24

I Told You So

Jenny wanted to snap a stinging retort to Branch's response to her praise. *How dare he declare he's the best?* She'd given him her admiration on a silver platter, and he should have thanked her. *It'll be a long time before I tell him he's good and brave and true—maybe never again. How foolish of me.*

Still furious with him, but needing to keep her mind focused, Jenny hissed at Branch, "Hurry!" as they sprinted through the sand. Branch ran past her. He clutched the metal handle of the boathouse door and tried to jerk it open. Jen reached over his hand and lifted the latch. The door creaked outward revealing a couple of canoes, old fishnets piled high in one corner, several wooden oars, a gasoline can, and that damp mildew smell that always lingers near the sea.

Surveying the paraphernalia inside, they stood quietly as their eyes adapted to the dim light. A troublesome thought wound its way to Branch's brain. He was reluctant to give it a voice because Branch knew he'd irritated Jen with his lack of proper appreciation for her praise, but he'd been too flustered to respond sincerely. He regretted that now. If his new theory proved reliable, maybe Jen would let him back in her good graces. He'd love to have her praise again.

"Jen, something's unusual in here. Things don't fit. Look around you. It's like a painting of the interior of a boathouse. Everything looks old, but there's no dust. It's all too neat. It reminds me of when we were looking at houses a couple years ago when we had to move again. We'd walk in, and everything was in its place. Nothing looked lived in, right?"

"Right. When people want you to rent their place, they hide the messes. You're supposed to believe only a perfect mom, a handsome dad, a precious cat, two fine kids, and a lovable dog live there. Apple pie baking in the oven, no dirty dishes, no garbage, no soap scum in the bathtub—no useless little brothers dropping water balloons over the banister."

"Right." Branch doubted his new idea was going to get him out of trouble, but he persisted. "Why is this staged like a movie set—real for this moment, but not looking at all lived in?"

Jenny peered into the room and observed its contents. She let go of her aggravation with Branch as she sensed a crawly spider sensation tickling her arms. Lowering her voice to a faint whisper, in case they were being heard and watched, Jenny studied the edges of the room, searching for anything that might be a listening device.

"Branch, keep talking. Make it sound like you're interested in that canoe over there. Talk about everything in here; pretend you're leading a tour or a field trip."

While Branch looked around and picked up several things, detailing their appearance out loud, Jenny pretended interest while she carefully studied items that might hide any secret devices. She wasn't sure she was clever enough to fool anybody watching or listening, but she could at least try.

She kept her voice a whisper. "Branch, see? There's no dust. I doubt boathouses ever get dusted. There should be dust. Lots of it."

Branch bit his tongue hard to keep from shouting, "I told you so!" He believed they were on to something, and he wanted to be her hero again. Branch would not mess it up this time so he could get back in Jen's Queendom as her Most Trusted Knight, no smudges on his armor, his lance intact.

25

Button, Button, Who's Got the Button?

Terrence, in the AstroSPAN office, was eager to get the gamers to safety. The room was quiet, except for his pencil tapping. His usual mantra failed to relax him. He realized they'd need to do something soon or risk the catastrophic event the designers warned about. He chose to bluff his way out of his despair, pretending he had an idea that might serve them well.

"Ralph, it's time."

"Time for what, Oh Magnificent One, Oh Solver of All Things Unsolvable, Oh Friend of the Friendless?"

Ralph was quite nervous. He played along with Terrence in case he had a brilliant solution, which Ralph believed impossible at this point.

"Time to summon help. To go directly to the Masters, admit we're out of ideas—way over our heads in figuring how to get the family to safety. We're beyond our level of expertise. We've had no AstroSPAN directives in three days. Tony betrayed us. Meg and Dave are caught up in a tornado of sorts. Jenny and Branch are stuck in a boathouse that's about to explode." Terrence trailed off, out of breath from spewing out his fears.

"What did you just say?" Ralph's mouth dropped open and his eyes widened at what he heard.

"What? What did I say?"

"You said Jenny and Branch are in a boathouse that's about to explode. How do you know that?"

"I don't know. It just popped out of my mouth. What's going on? Someone or something has taken over my thoughts, even my speech."

Ralph and Terrence stood silent for several moments, struggling to make sense of what had happened. They were supposed to be in complete control of the training game's activities, lessons, and results. At least they always had been until now. If Terrence spoke words he didn't plan to say, what's next? Who or what *was* in command?

Terrence's mantra now had special meaning for *both* of them.

We don't know everything about everything.

26

All Tied Up
At the Moment

Meg woke up to a nasty odor. *What is that? Oh, yeah, it's how our garage smells after a rain. Dave really needs to fix that leak that flows down the walls. I've been asking him, but he never has time. Too busy saving our planet, I guess.*

The minute she thought of Dave, Meg became fully awake. She realized she was curled up on a dirt floor. The tight straps on her wrists and ankles felt like leather. A piece of cloth covered her mouth. She could see only a few shadowy shapes in the darkness, but she was sure she was underground, in a basement room with no windows.

She swiveled her body, stretching out her

bound legs for leverage, attempting to reach any object nearby. Her feet touched a leg belonging to someone else. *Please let that be Dave. Please let him be okay.* She heard a groan, and her mind did a happy dance. She'd recognize that groan anywhere, even in the dim underground where mildew lives.

27

Out of Control

Branch scanned the main floor of the boathouse to look for anything helpful. He spotted a bump in the flooring and was about to show it to Jen when she signaled to him to move back by her.

"Hear that, Branch?"

Branch stood still to hear the hissing coming from the floor area he had just left. They tiptoed toward the bump, avoiding touching anything. Branch knelt and grabbed a circular metal pull-key, raising a hatch lid to reveal steep steps heading down. Jenny clutched the wood rim around the hatch and lowered her feet to the first step.

Branch usually followed Jen's lead at home, but now this seemed rather foolhardy because there was no light at all in that lower level, plus it smelled worse than the main floor mildew. But as the hissing grew louder, he knew he had to follow Jen in case she needed his help.

Jen reached the last step and slowly inched off the stairs onto a dirt surface, with Branch close behind. She hoped her eyes would adjust to the lack of light soon. The hissing sound increased until it leveled off to a steady, loud volume. Uncertain what it was or where it was coming from, three words stuck in her mind: *out of control.*

Branch stepped off the bottom step right behind Jen, thankful he could now touch her shoulder. Jenny was so glad Branch had not shut the hatch door above them, in case they needed to exit fast.

28

Let There Be Light

Just as Ralph heard Terrence mumble his mantra for the fifth repetition, he glanced over at the farthest observation monitor in the control office. He saw Branch lower himself onto the stairs inside the boathouse. Ralph crossed his hands in a timeout gesture to stop Terrence from repeating his mantra a sixth boring time and then pointed to the screen. Terrence turned around and tapped the Enlarge button on the keyboard. The computer responded quickly, zeroing in on Dave and Meg lying on the floor, not moving. Terrence and Ralph could see their shapes but could not assess their condition.

"Enough! They need our aid!"

Terrence knew they were not to interfere unless the players *asked* for help or a situation appeared entirely out of control. Ralph had wanted to apply their behind-the-scenes power for a while now, but he always waited for Terrence to lead.

Terrence made his decision based on one thing: the hissing sound. He had no clue what it was or its source. It was *not* part of their advance planning.

He hit the Control and L keys simultaneously. A blinding light engulfed the underground room. They saw Meg and Dave in the northwest corner—groggy, but awake now. The second the light blazed, Jenny and Branch took their first steps off the stairs and threw themselves face down on the floor.

Ralph and Terrence watched Jenny lift her head to see her parents bound and gagged in the corner. Branch sprang to action and in three strides catapulted himself to his parents and clutched at their bindings to loosen them. His efforts were useless. Their straps remained in place. No weak spots.

29

Best-Laid Plans

"Piece of cake! Told ya so," Tony said to the two evil ShrinkWithers in their Control Copter. He had waited a long time to get the AstroSPAN players in a group so they could be destroyed in one swoop. He had almost succeeded in the last game competition a year ago and had looked forward to this year's games, but he was left out of the planning sessions. He didn't know why. He worried about it constantly.

The ShrinkWithers nodded at Tony, then went back to observing their screens. They had been surprised to see the lights go on. They stared at the scene on the largest monitor. The ShrinkWithers spoke first. Tony always wondered why they spoke in unison. He'd gotten used to it over the years, but it was odd, really odd. They didn't look like robots, but they sure sounded like robots.

"Not sure we're all on the same page here. Check your playbooks; tell me what you think. Tony, I thought you wired that light to turn on only when the final Exit Expansion occurs. Why are they bathed in light right now?"

Tony needed time to think of an excuse. He was an expert in excuses and shifting blame.

"Dunno, Boss. Something must have shorted out. I checked everything three times. Should've worked like a dream." He spoke slowly, hoping to stall long enough to hatch an outstanding idea. It didn't help. He decided to try to distract them.

"Notice anything odd, Boss? That hissing sound. It's twice as loud as it was a minute ago."

"Yeah, sure is, and that makes us happy, very happy. Things are gonna get exciting real soon."

Tony realized they knew something he didn't.

30

Plan Sesame Seed

"**C**ut!"

The abrupt command from Terrence shocked Ralph. He had wanted to shout it himself for at least ten minutes, but he didn't feel right taking over from Terrence. Ralph watched Terrence, expecting him to give the next order specified in their training sequence, authorizing him to suspend the action on the set. Next, they would clear the dangers by a series of computer commands and avert catastrophe. He glanced at Terrence, waiting.

Terrence said nothing. He sat in front of his screen, arms limp, mouth open, no sound coming forth. He looked asleep, but his eyes were open, staring into space.

Ralph panicked. He had two options. Should he take control and complete the next step in the sequence? Or should he give Terrence a minute to recover? They had rehearsed emergency routines many times in their training, but today's bizarre events carried the immediate risk of failure and potential loss of life.

Ralph waited and counted to ten in his head. *One, two, three . . .*

Ralph didn't have time to finish the count. Before he could think *four*, Terrence recovered his wits and his voice and bellowed "Sesame Seed!" into the microphone.

31

When I Say Jump, You Say . . .

The minute Terrence shouted "Sesame Seed," Meg and Dave's leather straps broke apart. Dave sprang up and reached over toward Meg to help her stand. Meg beat him to it, jumping up promptly as her straps fell away. Branch grabbed for his mom, hugging her tightly. Jenny steadied Dad, and all four of them wobbled toward the stairs to escape.

The hissing grew louder. A giant metal canister rolled toward them, cutting off the path to the bottom of the stairs. A fiery balloon of steam escaped from the neck of the canister. Dad motioned for everyone to freeze. He realized he had merely a moment to figure out their course of action. Not knowing if the canister held toxic chemicals, he knew he needed to act fast to avoid a worst-case disaster—if it exploded.

Dad held out his hand and screamed, "Hang on tight!"

Branch grabbed Dad's hand, Mom clutched Branch's outstretched hand, Jenny gripped Mom's hand, and they all vaulted over the canister in perfect leaps, just high enough to clear it. They took the stairs two at a time and raced up through the hatch opening, across the main floor, and out the door, galloping toward the shoreline.

32

When In Need,
Try Sesame Seed

Ralph let his breath out slowly. His confidence returning, Terrence smiled and high-fived Ralph. As they observed the family escape the boathouse basement, it looked like all was right in their screen-world, no lives lost. Everyone was safe on the beach. Their Sesame Seed command had worked, coupled with Dave's quick response to the hissing canister. Terrence and Ralph relaxed as they saw everyone escape, corresponding to plan, according to their training.

Terrence gave Ralph a minute to check all his computer entries. When Ralph looked up and signaled "all complete," Terrence leaned over and whispered, "Now, Sesame Seed Two."

Ralph swiveled his chair toward Terrence, stunned upon hearing Sesame Seed Two.

"You out of your mind again, Terrence? What's Sesame Seed Two? What are you talking about? We've been trained together. There is no Part Two Sesame Seed."

"I've been tasked with the removal of the ShrinkWithers. I am the only one who has been given the information to carry out this battle. It was safer if only one of us knew, in case any of us were captured during this game session. They managed to break into our headquarters this time. They have accessed our players. Their greed and ignorance have done enough damage to our environment. If they are allowed to continue and win this battle for control, Earth and its people will not recover. Our resources will be gone, our air and water will remain polluted, our forests will disappear. Countries will no longer be able to protect their populations."

Ralph gripped his chair arms tightly as he tried to decide if Terrence was telling the truth and really had been given this responsibility alone. He knew the games they had designed and played over the years had the sincere mission of making life better for everyone, in order to bring peace and balance to world communities and all cultures. It was a huge goal that could be accomplished only with excellent education, common objectives, and the sharing of technical resources.

As Ralph weighed his decision, he knew there was only one answer. The ShrinkWithers were destructive. They must be removed.

"Let me know what you want me to do, Terrence. I'm with you. It's your call, now."

"It's our only choice, Ralph. Thanks for trusting me. Hold down the Control and Option and Caps Lock keys on your center keypad with your left hand, then type in SESAME SEED II with your right hand, all capital letters."

33

Gulp, Gulp, Gulp!

The family could hear a loud rumbling sound behind them as they ran, followed by a tremendous explosion that rocked the area. Dad shouted, "Join!"

They clasped hands again and raced away from the noise, aiming for the ocean's edge.

And then it began.

At first, the sand moved in slow waves, enormous dune-like areas rising and falling as the family sprinted toward the water. Branch and Jenny seemed not to notice. Being closer to the ground, their legs adapted easily to the movement of the earth underneath them.

Meg and Dave reacted first. On the next pulsing of the sand, Dave lost his balance and fell. Meg, running closely by his side, tripped over him when he fell into her.

As they rebounded upright, a giant blast of energy blew all four of them twelve feet in the air. They folded up their legs, clasped their hands around their knees, and somersaulted to a bumpy but safe stop as they landed. They jumped up quickly and hit the sand running—exactly like they had practiced in their training sequences.

Always alert, Dad kept checking behind them frequently. He was astonished to see that a gigantic crater had opened in the sand. The hole was growing at a fast rate, in all directions. The sky had suddenly filled with what appeared to be large fleets of helicopters and oval flying saucers. He had to keep turning around to see where he was going, so he didn't see the most unusual event at first. Next time he turned, he saw hundreds of helicopters swoop down to be swallowed by the crater. The flying saucers followed, large groups disappearing into the earth, no longer to be seen. He didn't want to distract Meg and the kids from their running, so he kept it to himself. Something serious was happening. He was glad they were able to keep in front of it.

* * *

Ralph watched Terrence as much as what was happening on their screens. Terrence looked calm and focused. Knowing that thousands of ShrinkWithers were at the controls of all those downed aircraft was disturbing. He thought he'd ask.

"Okay, Terrence, I didn't sign up for this level of destruction. I signed up for *saving*, not destroying. Even if they are the bad guys."

"And your point is?"

"Well, look at your screens. All those pilots have just been destroyed."

"Oops, forgot to tell you. There hasn't been time until now. Each aircraft is being pulled deep below the surface of the ground into gigantic spaceship containers. When each container is full, it shoots out into space, docking at a large space station, all pilots and crew still in their crafts and still alive. Remember, we also know now that seventy-five percent of the ShrinkWither forces are, as we suspected all along, mechanical robots. Only twenty-five percent are human, of sorts. Great care has been taken in the planning to show respect for our enemy and try to reeducate or reprogram."

34

NO

Now What?

When Dad turned around again, he was pleased to see the moving sand dunes had slowed down, the crater had closed over, and all the aircraft had completely disappeared. He motioned for everybody to halt about a hundred feet from the sea. It would be good to sit for a moment. While he was curious to know what had just happened with the crater and the aircraft, he could wait to find out when they were debriefed in a couple of weeks.

As they plopped down on the sand to catch their breath and wits, he feared they were out of options. They were on open land again, obvious targets. They saw no buildings, and the boathouse had been an ambush, so he couldn't be sure they'd be protected even if they found cover.

This break was a chance to share ideas. He knew Branch and Jenny expected their parents to have the best solutions to any dilemma, both in-game and out-of-game. But based on experience, he knew their kids had many solid and intuitive insights—just as clever as their parents, sometimes more so. He'd start with Jenny.

Dad waited for Jenny to catch her breath. He noticed her shoulders sagged more than usual. This year's game required super energy, day and night, with no rest between sessions. Jenny and Branch had never shown panic in the previous game, but this year's competition had greatly increased the practice hazards and created several truly dangerous situations. The ShrinkWithers had managed to gain access to the games, the contestants, and the AstroSPAN control tower. Everyone was on edge.

Again, Dave and Meg were rethinking the wisdom of their reasons for enlisting. It was one thing to put themselves in jeopardy in the beginning, but entirely another to place these burdens on their kids, no matter how talented and strong they were. Dave's thoughts were racing through his mind as he planned how to talk with Jenny and Branch to keep their spirits up.

Because of his years of involvement, Dave realized how threatening the rogue force behind the scenes was. It wasn't playing fair, it was not kid-friendly, and it was definitely sinister. Preparing for the final defeat of the ShrinkWithers in order to limit their destructive effects on our climate, resources, and vegetation was becoming a full-time mission.

Pockets of aware citizens and governments scattered across the globe were making plans and taking actions to curb the threat, but not everyone was on board with how fast some parts of Earth were being affected. He knew these games were a vital effort to draw out the ShrinkWithers, hoping to break through to their leaders before they managed to destroy major resources.

"Jennifer Elizabeth?" He expected to see Jenny's smile, acknowledging their longtime name game.

Jenny sat on the sand, hugging her knees, head down. She didn't look up when Dad spoke. Her lack of reaction made him sad and alarmed.

He glanced over at Branch, sprawled next to Mom, eyes half closed. He'd most likely pass out soon from exhaustion. Regret flooded through Dad. It's one thing to get tired spending long summer days playing sports, but much more difficult to try to save your parents from explosions and race across moving sand dunes. Branch wasn't even supposed to be on this venture. He should have had a couple more years to reach his prime, to grow and mature.

What have I done to my family?

Meg sensed Dave's conclusions as she leaned on his shoulder. Their thinking was usually so similar. She asked herself the same questions, had the same doubts. When she asked herself if the outcome justified the means, she came up with a firm "No."

35

Now You See Us,
Now You . . .

Dad allowed the family a few more minutes to rest. They had to act quickly or risk another capture, but today's challenges had worn them out. He continued checking in all directions for any more traces of movement or impending disaster. Thankfully, the air had calmed, and the sands had stilled. There was no opening where the crater had been. When he looked out to sea, he saw no clouds on a peaceful horizon, but he remained alert in case things changed. The kids looked so tired, he decided to wait before telling them what he had seen behind them while they were running.

It seemed a long time had passed since they

had been home, and while it was always wonderful spending time with his family, this year's TriTopTechRun had not been what he had expected. They'd barely finish one challenge when another popped up. Remembering back to the designing days, he knew there were many things not fitting their original plan. He expected to have a lot to say at their post-game debriefing sessions. He intended to advise everybody to speak up and leave nothing out, including their many questions and fears.

"Jenny—" Before Dad could ask her what they should do to reach the sea, a powerful magnetic attraction grabbed them. Off they went again.

"Da-a-a-d-d-d . . ." Branch's voice faded as a force lifted him upside down and pulled him toward the ocean.

Each of them suffered the same lift and whoosh. They were moving so fast, no words were clear, only their screams could be heard.

Jenny set her mind to super-distance vision and immediately spotted the enemy's Renegade Amphibian Vehicle a mile ahead of them, streaming over the sea. At the pace they were being transported toward it, they'd reach it in less than two minutes. Using all her energy to resist the force of the magnetic pull, she cupped her hands together to show Mom her intention to use her teleportation power to create an invisible wrap around them and transport them back to land.

Only one problem. Teleportation usually took close to two minutes. They didn't have two minutes.

Focus. Focus. Jenny's eyes glazed over, her body stiffened, she clenched her teeth and snapped, "Now!"

Jenny had never felt so alive. A massive power surge rushed through her, raising her spirits and her courage. She was not frightened. She could think with lightning speed, and she was confident she'd be able to carry out their safe escape.

Her parents and Branch disappeared in an instant, and in forty-five seconds all four of them landed on a soft gray rubber raft heading up the coast, at least two miles away from the vehicle sent to capture them. As each one landed on the deck, they lost their invisibility.

Jenny grabbed the tiller, glad it required only her slight touch to steady it as they sped away. It was under an automatic navigation system. The raft's motor purred gently, but it exhibited unusual velocity, unlike any watercraft she'd used before.

Everything was happening so fast they had little chance to think. Branch needed to let out some nerves and shouted, "About time they came! What took so long?"

36

Water, Water
Everywhere

Once he realized they were all safely on the rescue raft, Dad checked Jenny to be sure she was ready to lead them if another challenge occurred. She appeared to have recovered her energy, which was odd because she was not in top form before she teleported them from the land to the rescue pontoon. He reached across the tiller and gave her a big hug. She responded with her broad smile, showing she was okay.

He made a split-second decision. He decided it was time to figure a way to close out their participation in this season's game, whether or not the AstroSPAN Masters agreed. He couldn't expose his kids to further risk. There had been severe threats to their lives this time, no fun, several injuries, and odd control factors. Even worse were the minimal communications with the Guides and the ShrinkWithers' intrusions. Watching his family face real danger was something he never wanted to see again. He held Meg close as he spoke to Jenny.

"Jennifer Elizabeth?"

"Yes, Dad?"

"Are you thinking what I'm thinking?"

"If you're saying it's time to go home and fix that leak in the garage, I'm with you, Dad. Anybody else notice how water always plays a large role in our lives?"

Branch was so tired he didn't say one word about Jenny's joke. *Hilarious, Jen.*

Acknowledgments

Game Over, Shrink Withers! is the product of years of learning and interacting with so many loving and talented family, friends, and cohorts. My unending gratitude goes to my children Leigha, Michael, and Michelle, and my grandchildren, and to hundreds of teachers and students and school staff—you are all amazing. My decade with Off Campus Writers Workshop (the longest continuous writing group in the country) has provided an endless source of inspiration with dedicated writers.

Special thanks to author and writing teacher Joan Dempsey for her expert guidance for my book in its early stages. Fellow writer Maureen O'Grady motivated this project and kept me going as we downed hot mugs of coffee, writing at libraries, bookstores, and restaurants. I cherish the unwavering longtime support from my multi-genre critique group members—Barry, Brenda, Buzzie, Richard, Estelle, Judy, Kelley, Lyle, and Peter—and my delightful Society of Children's Book Writers and Illustrators (SCBWI) critique group—Kim, Nicole, Alex, Lesley, Leslie, Bill, and Wiggy. You are all such fun and talented writers!

There are not enough words to thank my

editor, Kelley Chikos. A teacher and author herself (Trickle-Down Teaching: A Lighthearted Romp Through the Minefield of Your Rookie Year), she wields her sharp red-pencil knowledge with a kind hand and provides "literary bowling bumpers" to keep me within the writing lanes and always laughing.

My artist granddaughter, Samantha Haubrich, took a few words of description for the book's contents and magically drafted wondrous images for the cover and chapter headings. Wow! Just wow! Her sister, Maya, a college freshman who devours fiction, served as a beta reader starting at age fourteen (on swim practice rides) and shared great writing advice: "Don't escape a scene so quickly; slow down and expand the moments." Many thanks to their sister, Rebecca, and brother, Max, both excellent writers, for their faith and encouragement as they cheered me along. I owe all of them (including parents Michelle and Steve) thanks for years of exercise climbing bleachers to watch their swim meets, which inspired the swimming sequences in the "bubble" chapters. And I am so grateful for their perky kid comments, stolen from their growing-up years. Always beware what you say. You may end up on a page in a book one day!

I am delighted with the feedback from my recent young beta readers: Connor, Charlie, Ray, Millie, Conrad, Eileen, and grandchildren Rivka and Zev. May you always find good books to keep you entertained and informed. Thank you all for your help. Hooray for Honorary Team AstroSPAN!

The dedicated guidance of publisher Alexa Haddock Bigwarfe (Write/Publish/Sell), along with her outstanding writing workshops and network building strategies, has led me on an outstanding adventure with her expert team of Nancy Cavillones, Sarah O'Dell, Cayce LaCorte, and Raewyn Sangari.

About the Author

Sarah Schwarcz thrives on keeping it real, with a touch of magic and fantasy, making connections with people and ideas, and building community with writers and readers. She always keeps her eyes open and her heart full of page-turners for her life and her writing. Her favorite place is a classroom, sharing ideas with the greatest minds—children!

She had great fun writing this adventure filled with humor and quirky magic. Game Over, ShrinkWithers is on a mission to raise middle graders' awareness of the need to speed up our care and conservation of the world's resources. Family plays a major role in her life and in the novel's events. The group of young beta readers, ages 8-12, already report the story is "cool and relatable, with cliffhanger chapters." Let's hope Earth wins!

Sarah holds a Bachelor of Arts in English and French and a Master of Arts in Education Administration. As a teacher (Volta School, Chicago; West Oak Middle School, Mundelein, Illinois) and principal (Solomon and Sauganash Schools in Chicago Public Schools) and assistant high school principal (Ida Crown Academy, Chicago), she designed and taught multiple curriculum areas, specializing in Literature, Science, and Social Studies. Along with enhancing regular and gifted programs, Sarah introduced and piloted strong Inclusion programming for special education students, making sure all children in her schools received outstanding learning opportunities. With Kohl's Children's Museum, she designed and directed Kids Convention, one of the first computer-interactive programs for fifty-two Chicagoland schools.

Just like the character Branch, who wrote himself into this book early on, Winston, Sarah's ten-pound miniature wire-haired dachshund insisted on being included in her bio since he commands her home fort. (Shush! Please don't tell Winston he's not a Great Dane!)

Connect with Sarah:
www.sarahrayschwarcz.com
www.pearlsandknots.com
Instagram: sarahrayschwarcz
Facebook: SarahRaySchwarczAuthor

CPSIA information can be obtained
at www.ICGtesting.com
Printed in the USA
LVHW020844270921
698784LV00001B/7

9 781734 196825